THE CARPENTER'S SECRET

NOAH HARRIS

The Carpenter's Secret

BOOK 1
FAMILY SECRETS

NOAH HARRIS

language and may be considered offensive to some readers. Please don't read if you are under eighteen.

PROLOGUE

*L*ater, when Dean really thought about it, everything that had happened in his life could be blamed on that single piece of paperwork. A lot of change in life could be attributed to one seemingly harmless object or event, he knew that. Yet, the events that followed this one particular act could never have been predicted, not even by the most skilled of psychics.

Being an insurance adjuster wasn't exactly what you'd call an exciting life. It paid the bills, and the benefits weren't anything to scoff at: steady hours, decent pay, and no one questioned what you did when the subject of work came up over cocktails. His co-workers weren't terrible, but they weren't interesting either. It was dry, long, thankless work that just happened to pay the bills, and then some.

Dean Matthews hadn't pictured his life turning out that way. While he had certainly kept a backup plan in mind when choosing his college courses, his original major had been in agriculture. He took minors in animal care subjects, and his farming knowledge and first-hand experience in the fields meant his career path had been all set. His parents had not been particularly supportive of his decision, but what could they do? He was determined to live the life of a farmer, and with his expanding knowledge and his degree getting closer each day, farming was all he thought he'd ever do.

His grandfather had been a farmer his whole life.Every summer as a child and teenager, Dean spent a considerable amount of time with his grandfather. As he grew older, he had less time to spend there, but those few experiences had inevitably led to his decision to study agriculture. His grandfather had been the only person to support Dean's ambition, though he had a good laugh at the notion of going to college and studying it. Dean was certain that the only reason his father hadn't chided him for it was the fact that between financial aid and scholarships, he wasn't having to pay a dime for Dean's time at school.

Dean hadn't felt like he'd come into his own until college. He enjoyed independence and freedom on campus and he could go to the gym whenever he wanted. He wasn't particularly well-built, but he kept himself in shape. Summers on the farm had given him an appreciation for hard work and the strength required to do it. His hair and eyes were both brown, so dark that they were almost black. Along with his naturally darker skin colour—thanks to his Native American ancestors—all he was missing was the "tall" of "tall, dark, and handsome." It didn't bother him too much being on the shorter side of average. His dark features leant him a serious look, and his handsome face just added to the appearance.

The change came when Dean's parents suddenly died. They were the victims of a rough storm, slick roads, and an oncoming semi. Getting through the funeral proved easier than anyone expected, Dean included. He was so busy dealing with their affairs that he hardly had time for grief. They had not been terribly wise with their money, and he had barely managed to cover funeral expenses with his father's insurance payout. He covered their debt with the sale of the house, his childhood home. His grandfather had been the one to bear the burden of his grief, when he had finally paid the last of the bills. The old man put his own grief aside to comfort Dean...all that remained of his now-lost daughter.

After he settled the estate, Dean hadn't had much of a legacy left to him. The money left over was just enough to continue school for about a year and that was all. With that in mind, he made a tough decision. Agriculture was no longer a viable option. So, he changed his major and worked his ass off to get himself the degree that led him to his current career. He could, at least, say that the choices he made were right, rather than struggling and probably failing to make ends meet pursuing his love of agriculture. As it turned out, he found himself a job quickly after finishing college, even in a struggling market. Although disappointed with the loss of his dream, he felt alright about his choices, and was ready to step up and follow his new path.

Life, however, had taken even that small satisfaction from Dean when his grandfather suddenly passed away. It was a heart attack. Dean was told that it had probably been so severe that no one could have saved him, even if they had been right there. The worst of it was, he had only been found when the mailman got worried, after missing him at the mailbox for three days in a row. The last of Dean's family, a man he loved dearly, had suffered—probably scared and in pain—and had died alone.

Dean's grief at the loss of his grandfather was sharper and far more agonizing than he had felt at the death of his parents. A group of local men and women had been placed in charge of his grandfather's affairs. They funded Dean's trip to attend the service. His grandfather's lawyer dealt with all other matters and, after handing Dean a sealed packet with written instructions on it, sent him on his way to grieve alone. His grief was too much and too raw to be addressed immediately so, with no family left, and no place to call home, he retreated from it all and threw himself into his work.

Six years as an adjuster had proven to be utter hell. Although the work was predictable, the office was a thankless and spiteful place to work. You could only take being treated like dirt so many times before it began to get to you. His boss—demanding, petty, and way too good at getting away with things—was an utter monster to work for.

The rest of Dean's life seemed set to follow the path his career had taken. Sure, he was reasonably comfortable in an apartment with a car of his own. But none of it truly provided him with much beyond a place to retreat to and something to get around in. At 27, his life appeared to be quite normal, stable, and perhaps even envied. In truth, he hated it. That hate grew each year, like an itch at the back of his skull that he could never scratch, no matter how hard he tried. He had a boring, soul-sucking job, a friendless existence, and an apartment filled with mundane responsibilities: a semi-feral cat, a dopey boxer-ish mix of a dog, and several plants that he cared for almost obsessively. His calm and measured approach to life was catching up with him, and he was beginning to understand why, after a decade or two of this sort of thing, some people simply went crazy.

He had made a few friends over the years, but he never managed to keep them for long. They had been largely reduced to occasional texts or half-hearted invites to some gathering or another, none of which he followed through on. Connecting with people had always been hard for him before, and it had become even worse since losing his whole family within the span of a year.

He didn't mind the occasional hook up or casual fling, but that seemed to be the norm these days. Even the few short relationships he had weren't as committed as he originally thought and he ended up being cheating on. Other people found flaws in him that they ultimately couldn't put up with, so they left. He was too quiet, too distant, gave too much attention to his plants and his pets and not enough to people. His struggle to connect with fellow humans consigned him to being friendless, boyfriend-less, and totally sexless.

He couldn't imagine what his life might have spiraled downwards into had he not accidentally knocked a box from the top shelf of his closet. After grumbling and rubbing the lump on his head, he spotted the packet his grandfather's lawyer had given him years ago. He'd never opened it. The instructions on the packet were clear enough, the time to open it was not when he'd received it. He had trusted his grandfather enough to obey the words written on it:

For when you regret the road not taken.

The note brought a faint smile to his face when he read it again. It had been over six years since he'd stowed it out of sight. It referred to a discussion they'd had long ago over a Robert Frost poem. His grandfather was fond of interpreting the poem as being about taking risks and being bold. Dean believed it to be more wistful and regretful than anything. They'd had more than a few debates on it over the years. This had been his grandfather's last jab at him, a little acknowledgment of Dean's point of view.

Clearly, it was intended for a time in his life, such as this, when everything seemed wrong and mixed up. He really had been regretting his choice to live a normal, stable lifestyle. Being predictable and safe had done nothing but bring him banality and misery. He had no idea what his grandfather thought about the future, but perhaps the man's wisdom had been greater than Dean had given him credit for.

Inside the packet was the answer: legal papers detailed the transfer of ownership of the family farm to Dean. Every piece of property, the machinery, and even contacts that Dean could use were detailed. Everything he would need to get started was there as well, including the name and number of the lawyer. Dean turned over each page, the details of the transfer blurring as his eyes misted, then he stopped on the last page. Beneath blocks of legal text was his grandfather's familiar scrawl:

Dean,

This land has been in our family for generations. Even before it was claimed by settlers. The tribe that lived on this land before the settlers came runs in your very blood. It is more than just looks, little though there is. You have their soul in your blood, boy, just as sure as I did.

I always thought that you would be the one to take over the care of this land for me in the end. I'm hoping if life doesn't make you happy where you are, you'll find your way here instead. I know you will find the peace here that you used to have as a youngster.

The old tribe used to believe that the souls of their ancestors sometimes stayed on their land somewhere to watch over their families. If that's true, I'll be here when you need me. You only need to look.

Be seeing you again my boy,
Grandpa Christopher

Years of unexpressed grief suddenly poured out of Dean with a violence that scared him. Sorrow and grief tore him up inside. He curled up on the couch, unable to stem the tide of tears and hoarse sobs. Never had he been more thankful for the company of his strange mutt and crazy cat as they cuddled up with him while he mourned.

When he had recovered enough to wipe his face clean and breathe properly, he eyed his phone. For the first time in ages, he didn't pause to weigh the pros and cons. He did not measure the cost, nor did he predict his odds of success. Instead, he just called the lawyer.

In his mind the "road not traveled" awaited him, offering everything he had dreamed of before his life had been turned upside down by the untimely death of his parents. Sometimes he wondered what he would have said back then if he had been told what the future held? But that wasn't how life worked, and now he was looking forward to a new beginning...one that would start the moment he set foot on the land he hadn't seen in six long years.

1

———

"Oh hell," Dean muttered as he stepped down from the cab of the truck, barely noticing as Jax, his crazy mutt, darted out of the truck in a bid for freedom.

"I know. It's looked better," the lawyer, Davis, said as he walked up to Dean with a sympathetic expression.

That was a colossal understatement, Dean thought. As he stood there, cat carrier in hand and surveyed his surroundings, he agreed. It had looked better... a lot better. The last six years had really done a number on the place. His sense of foreboding began at the rusty gate at the bottom of the drive and had only grown stronger the closer he got. The dirt path leading up to the house was rough and overgrown, making it difficult to pass. The place had been taken over by plants, and he'd been told that sworkmen had already cleared a few trees that had fallen across the path. He was still unprepared for the sight that met him when they broke from the tree-lined path and he was finally able to see his new home. Immediately his chest began to ache.

The once bright, white house with red shutters and trim was a shadow of its former self. The small flecks of red paint that remained were flaking and the rest had paled to a washed out pink. The white had fared no better, it was peeling and cracked and no longer even looked white. Having been exposed to the elements for quite some time, it had turned to a dull, dusty brown. The porch, wrapping around the sides of the house, sagged and looked decidedly unsafe. Nothing seemed irreparable from the outside, at least nothing that would prove too expensive to put right. It was simply an old place that hadn't known a loving hand in some time.

The fencing that once ran stoutly from the house to the nearby farm buildings was in worse shape though. The few sections that remained were ready to crumble or fall apart. The path itself was no longer well-worn and neatly trimmed. It had become badly overgrown as nature reasserted itself in the absence of man.

At first glance, Dean thought that the large building housing the farm equipment and chicken coops would probably have to be completely rebuilt. Two of the four coops had partially collapsed, and the other two looked only a good gust of wind away from doing the same. The main barn had been built with the same care and quality as the house, however. While the dark brown paint had been all but stripped away, the structure still looked stable enough. The only work it would need would be the roof and anything inside that had deteriorated.

The fields beyond the buildings had disappeared completely, they were so overgrown with vegetation that he had to call upon his memories just to visualise them. The fields his grandfather had worked so tirelessly in were essentially gone, fields he himself had worked and played in as a child on so many hot, summer days. The state of the whole place saddened him. The contrast between his memories and the stark reality in front of him caused more pain than he could say.

Somehow, he didn't believe all this had happened in the six years the farm had sat vacant. His grandfather had been getting on in years before he died and it wasn't too difficult to imagine that he had been unable to manage to keep the place up and running. Dean regretted that his grandfather hadn't reached out to him before he passed, though he didn't know what he would have been able to do back then. Anything would have been better than letting the old man live out his last days with the place falling apart around him.

"It certainly has," he murmured finally. Davis had patiently waited as his client took it all in. Dean could only manage a half-hearted smile when the man patted his shoulder. He had been ready for the place to require some work, but he wasn't prepared for the reality of it.

"It will take a great deal of work and care," Davis said. "Now, I do, however, know a few local people who would be glad to help, if you wish. Considering your grandfather's standing in the community, they won't charge you too much. He was well-loved, and many of us would like to see the old place up and running again."

Dean could only nod in response, unable to find the words to agree. Summers spent growing up on the farm with his grandfather, guaranteed he wasn't averse to or unfamiliar with the amount of hard work that would be required. He wasn't confident that he would be able to repair the place properly himself. He was no carpenter, even with the knowledge he had picked up over the years. The smaller repairs and aesthetic changes he could handle on his own, with time. Everything else would require someone with more experience and skill.

"I'll be sure you get the information then," Davis said

after a moment. With one last pat on the back and another sympathetic look before walking back to his car, he drove away, leaving Dean alone.

He couldn't say how long he stood there holding the cat carrier, staring at the worn porch and the equally weathered front door, before finally moving inside. The steps creaked dangerously under his feet as he walked to the door. It squealed loudly as he pushed it open, it was as dilapidated as everything else so far. Light from the afternoon sun streamed into the dusty entry hall.

Relief flooded over him as he glanced around. Whatever the state of the outside of the house, the interior had fared considerably better. Dirt and dust lay on every surface as Dean walked further into the house, yet everything stood undisturbed. The old tables and chairs rested under a blanket of dust, as did the light fixtures that hung from above. He tested each one as he walked from room to room. Davis had said that they had checked everything over to make sure it was all functioning and safe, but he had to see it for himself.

"We're home, Nix," he told his cat, setting the carrier down in the hallway. The multicolored cat made her own break for freedom the moment he opened the carrier door. He was sure she would sulk for days after being stuck in the truck for hours. Jax was still happily bounding around outside having never known so much space to run round in. Dean had always been good about making sure he was well-exercised, but he knew this was a different world and Jax was definitely more pleased with things than Nix appeared to be.

Dean stood in the hallway, taking in the faded wallpaper, the dusty fireplace in the living room, and the electric wall torches. Even beneath the layers of dirt and dust, he could easily recognize the house he remembered from his childhood. The curtains would have to be replaced, and he would most likely have to get rid of the old wallpaper, despite feeling quite nostalgic about it. The banister rail leading to the next floor may need to be replaced, or at least reinforced. Davis had warned him that the kitchen appliances would need to be upgraded, so he already had those on order.

The stairs creaked a bit as he climbed slowly to the second floor. The upper hallway ran either way on both sides of the stairs. To his left, there was the bedroom that had once been his mother's, then the guest room and bath he had used on his visits. There was nothing in the guest room save for the bed, the frame of which still looked strong. He would have to make sure to get the pictures and small items that had once adorned the room out of storage and put back in their rightful places.

From the handmade dream-catcher that had hung over his bed, to the deep colored paintings that depicted some of the strangest scenes, Dean had always taken comfort in anything to do with his family history. He would lie in bed, stroking the leather strings and beads of the dream-catcher, studying each painting before falling asleep: the shadow-faced man who walked, rather than fought, with wolves; a group of strangely-dressed men, dancing around a fire that blazed inside the circle they formed. He would bring them all back and put them where he could see them again. Each item held memories he wanted to keep hold of and cherish.

At the other end of the hallway were his grandfather's rooms. His grandmother had died shortly after Dean was born, so he couldn't remember anyone living here save the old man. The first door was his grandfather's office. The old desk and thick bookcases still stood, immune to the ravages of time. They were as empty as the rest of the house, and he idly wondered what had happened to all the old books, papers and ledgers.

His grandfather's bedroom was the next door down the hall. As much as he felt the hum of nostalgia for his old room, he knew that this would be his room now. The temptation to keep it as a shrine was strong. Yet, his grandfather had passed the entirety of this place onto him, in letter and spirit. It was the largest bedroom by far, the room meant for the owner of the house and the land that lay beyond it. He was troubled by the idea of claiming it as his own, yet he knew full well what the old man would say at that.

"You're the man of this house now. You can't take care of it right if you don't make it yours, Dean," he recited to the empty room, the words resonating with his best impersonation of the booming voice he remembered so well. Yes, that sounds about right. The back of his eyes suddenly stung as he smiled, knowing that his grandfather would have lectured him endlessly about the responsibility he had to the place and to the land, steeped in history. "I'll try my best, Grandpa," he murmured to the empty room, running his fingers down the bedpost. "You can be sure of that."

2

No matter how hard he had worked on this farm when he was younger, he'd never known anything approaching this level of exhaustion. It was difficult to believe that only a few shorts days had passed since his return. The first day's non-stop flurry of activity had led to this moment, where he found himself sitting on the couch taking a quick break.

The new appliances had been installed and stood gleaming among the antique wood cabinets and trim that was probably older than his parents would have been. It turned the kitchen into a strange mix of both old and new. His own furniture had also been added to the house, though he'd kept his grandfather's large antique dining set. As nice as his own set had been, nothing could beat a hand-carved, solid redwood table and matching chairs. He wasn't quite sure where his grandfather had managed to get enough redwood to make the set, but it was beautiful and he wasn't getting rid of it.

Other than lugging in his own furniture and appliances, and bringing in box after box of his things, most of his effort

had been spent on cleaning. He was glad he'd had the fore-
sight to buy cleaning supplies in bulk before he'd arrived at
the property. The first couple of days he had scoured the
place from top to bottom. Now with every speck of dirt
swept away, there wasn't a dust bunny in sight. The light
fixtures gleamed and the freshly polished floors glowed in
the late afternoon light.

His grandfather's belongings that had once decked the
halls and floors of this place, had been removed from
storage and delivered to the farm. Dean was still in the
process of putting them back and rearranging them a bit.
He'd spent most of the day placing things out on display,
both his grandfather's and his own. As he worked, he slowly
brought things back into the light and gradually filled the
house.

Despite his initial reticence at the prospect of running
the house, he had taken to it with enthusiasm. Thinking of
what his grandfather would have wanted had been a great
motivator. Now, he felt a fresh sense of freedom in bringing
life back to the old place. He could almost feel the old man
over his shoulder at times, watching with approval. Nearly
every generation of his family had stamped their own mark
on the place; the house and property changing slightly with
each warden of the homestead. It was his turn now, and
there was a great sense of empowerment and responsibility
in doing so.

Being in charge was exhausting. Part of the reason he
had been so intent on getting the house set up and comfortable had been the season. With winter finally breaking, the
planting season was quickly coming up. Once the house was
ready, he would have to move straight onto the fields to see
what he could do with them. He was more than thankful for
his lifelong obsession with agriculture and his grandfather's

instruction, knowing that he was going to have to face that task... and soon.

The costs were racking up quickly, and the equipment needed to get the farm up and running wasn't going to be cheap. Then came buying and caring for the animals as well. The farm was by no means large, but it could certainly sustain whatever family was living on it. Being by himself, he was pretty sure he could manage to live comfortably enough. Thanks to his saving habits, he had enough money to get everything the farm needed. He even had a good chance of making it when he had to tide himself over the winters. Plus, he wasn't completely alone.

Deliveries had been fairly consistent. The workers coming in and out of the house to check over the new furnace and appliances had hung around for a while to chat. Then there were the neighbors and townsfolk who had taken to stopping by as well. Davis had warned him that they probably would, so he hadn't been surprised when the first one had shown up on his doorstep.

Mrs. Williams was one of the people he remembered from his childhood. Despite his time away, she hadn't seemed to age very much. Her thick white hair only served to enhance the brightness of her blue eyes as she stood on his front porch. She had praised his return, applauded the work he had already completed, complimented him on how handsome he had become, and glorified just about everything else under the sun. She had also made sure to drop off plenty of food, which now occupied most of the space in his fridge. He was pretty sure there was enough cobbler and casserole in there to feed a family of twelve for a month. She had finally left with a promise to visit him again, saying, "I can see you're busy. Your grandpa must be smilin' down on you from up above. It's so good to see you, Dean."

Mr. Williams had shown up a few hours later. He was considerably less effusive with his praise than his wife but complemented the work Dean was doing. He had quietly strolled around the property after that and then left with a friendly wave and an invitation to come for dinner any time. Their neighbors, Mr. and Mrs. Sommers, had shown up a few hours afterward, bringing their own chatter and praise, as well as even more food. They hadn't stayed very long either, proclaiming they didn't want to be underfoot. With another invitation for dinner, they waved themselves off and left.

After that visitors stopped by for a quick hello and to thank Dean for coming back. It seemed there had been more love for this place and his grandfather than he had ever realized. Some simply stopped at the gate and waved, watching Dean work for a little while before passing on. Eventually, he would have to contend with all of these people again, to see familiar faces and perhaps others that he didn't remember very well from his childhood. The sense of thanks and community, however, was heartwarming.

The constant flow of people added to his exhaustion, making him grateful for the moment of peace he was currently enjoying. His break on the couch was the first real quiet time he'd allowed himself indoors, at least during daylight hours. Though the day was warmer than recently, it still wasn't quite warm enough to sit out on the porch and enjoy the afternoon. Instead, he sat, well, sprawled really, on his couch. Nix had ventured out now that everyone was gone. So, content with his glass of lemonade, another gift from a well-wisher, Dean watched the spry cat explore the room. It was her home as well, and now with the strangers gone it was only fair that she should have the run of the place for a little while. Jax had run himself ragged and was slumped in a nearby armchair, snoring heavily.

The soothing noises from the dog were broken by a firm knock on the door. They all jumped at the sudden intrusion on their quiet moment and Jax bounded to the door with a series of happy barks. Dean was a little slower, and considerably more graceful about getting off the couch. He repressed a sigh, dreading another well-wisher with even more food that he wouldn't be able to put a dent in. He was thankful for all the company, to be sure, but he would have appreciated a longer interval of peace and quiet. Such moments would be few and far between while he worked to get the place up and running.

"One moment!" he called as he shut Jax in the dining room. The last thing he needed was for the excited dog to take out some poor, good-hearted old lady with a casserole dish. Whatever breeds had been mixed with the boxer hadn't granted him any grace or sense of dignity.

What greeted him this time however, was not another neighbor. The man at the door was a good bit taller than him, which didn't mean much when you were Dean's height. He was well built, shoulders squared and arms muscled. The man's well-tanned skin made his hazel eyes seem brighter, and his head was topped by a wild tangle of light brown hair. Dean caught the scent of sawdust and earth that hung about him, almost like cologne.

"H-hi," Dean stammered as the man grinned a greeting. Dean was flustered. What in all hell was wrong with him? The guy was... well, he was definitely hot. It was only then that he noticed the small tool chest in the man's hand and realized he must be a workman sent up here as a result of one of the half-dozen calls he'd made in the past day. That explained the man's body too, a body built by labor and labor alone.

"Heya, you Dean?" The man looked at him quizzically, cocking his head slightly like a large puppy. The smile on his face faltered a little as he took in the smaller man. Dean could see the puzzlement and quickly worked to school his features into something a little less dopey. He was probably gaping like a moron, and the man appeared a little concerned.

"That's me," he said, proud that he kept the heat that was rolling around his gut from flushing across his face.

"I'm Mikael, Mikael Reed," the man said. Dean found himself liking the name immediately and watched the man's mouth as he pronounced the syllables carefully. 'Me-kell,' spoken in such a way that suggested he was used to other people mispronouncing it. Dean would even bet that it was a reflex from a childhood spent listening to people getting his name wrong.

"Nice to meet you, Mikael." He was careful to pronounce the name correctly, while offering his hand. From the man's smile and the vigorous way he shook Dean's hand, he was pretty sure he'd pronounced it right. "What can I do for you?"

"Hm, oh!" Mikael laughed. "Sorry, my head must be somewhere else. Uh, I'm the carpenter you asked for."

"Oh, I was expecting..." He trailed off, realizing what he was going to say might have been a little offensive.

"Someone older?" Mikael grinned, not at all bothered by the idea.

"A little... yeah," Dean admitted sheepishly.

"Don't worry, been building stuff since I could hold a hammer. Old Man Wright wouldn't have sent me out here if he didn't think I could hack it."

Dean smiled back, a little shyer than the other man. "Sorry, didn't mean to doubt you. You just seem a little young for someone who's supposed to know his way around a hammer and nails, I guess."

"Pfft, I'm twenty-five," the man snorted. "More than old enough to be past apprentice-level by big city standards."

The man wasn't much younger than him, but he didn't remember him from his childhood. He thought he would have recognized most of the people around his age that were still left in town.

"Twenty-five, huh? Don't remember seeing you around when I was younger."

"Oh that's right! Old Man Wright said you grew up around here, didn't he?" The man spoke as he examined the porch, poking and tapping at random. "But yeah, you wouldn't have. I'm from the Grove, so I didn't really see much of the town till I was older."

"Oh," was all Dean could manage. The Grove was short for The Shadow grove Settlement. He recalled that it was technically a part of the county, but it wasn't considered part of the town, which marked them as outsiders. Opinions of the place had been relatively split down the middle. Some considered the small settlement, only accessible by a single dirt road that ran through the woods, to be more than a little strange. Residents of the small enclave were reclusive. It was rumored that none of them owned a phone, so even those who didn't mind the settlers from The Grove thought they were peculiar. He'd never met anyone from there until now, though, only having heard the rumors, or the passing distasteful comments, depending on the person in question.

"Not a fan?" Mikael asked, finally eyeing him carefully, as if expecting that Dean might jump him from behind.

Dean shrugged, a little uncomfortable now. "Can't say.

Honestly I never really knew anyone from there before. I was mostly only here in the summer, anyway. But Grandpa always said y'all were good people, and I never knew him to be wrong about folks."

"He said that, huh? My daddy said he was a good man. I never got to really meet him, myself, though I saw him now and again when I was younger. He was one of the only people who'd come out there."

That was news to Dean. He'd never known his grandfather to go to The Grove, and he'd never heard the neighbors or even his parents mention it either. It wasn't exactly the easiest place to get to. With it being in the heart of the nearby woods, the path there was infamous for slowing down even the most durable vehicles. The people of The Grove didn't want visitors, anyway. Then again, Dean could sympathize. With the kind of reputation The Grove had, they probably didn't want people coming to gawk or stare.

"Yeah, so is it just the porch and the barn?" Mikael asked, seemingly oblivious to Dean being lost in his thoughts.

"Oh, no, there's that, plus a few other things that need work. Here, I'll show you."

Starting with the banister rail on the main stairs, he moved through the house showing Mikael the stairs leading to the basement. He hadn't really bothered with anything down there after the first day when he'd tried to see how the stairs had fared over the years. The cracking sound that came from the second step had been enough to tell him that perhaps someone more qualified should take a look first.

Most of the work needing to be done was outside. The fence that ran around the property would probably need to be completely restored. The barn needed more than a few things done to it, and like the house, would need the roof patched and mended in places. The other buildings were all in need of various repairs. Mikael took all of this into consideration, stopping to look at each project that Dean showed him.

"Have a good memory?" Dean asked as he watched the man consider the equipment shed carefully. Not once had he seen Mikael take a single note on any of this. Considering how meticulous he himself was about keeping track of things, he found it strange that the other man wrote nothing down.

"Nah. If I were taking measurements, I'd jot 'em down. But I don't need them yet for something like this." Mikael again cocked his head in that endearing way. "I can get some good deals on lumber though, so even with all of this, it shouldn't be too bad. Any place you want me to start?"

Dean nodded toward the equipment shed immediately. "Out there and then the barn... and after that probably the porch. I think everything else can wait. Nobody but me to worry about, so you can hold off on the interior of the house. The porch though... I don't want any guests falling through my front porch, and it sounds like it's about to give out at any moment."

Mikael laughed. "Yeah, it's definitely seen better days, I'll give you that much. We've got enough stuff back at the Old Man's place to get the shed all done for you. That'll give me time to order the rest of the lumber we'll need, then I can get started on the barn. All in all, you're looking at a few weeks work."

Dean understood that the carpenter was trying to subtly and politely inform him that the cost was going to be significant. Even if it was just the one man, the material costs alone were likely to be a pretty penny. Dean didn't have much choice in the matter, since he needed most of the work done to get this place back in working order. The rest was simply for the sake of preserving the memory of this place properly, which he felt was also important.

"No worries," Dean said. "I have quite a nest egg saved up, so it shouldn't be a problem."

"Ain't city living pretty expensive? You must have had quite the job before you came out here, if you could save up that much."

Dean laughed. "Not really. I just didn't do much. A bit hard to burn through money when you don't spend it. I like to think that on some level, I was subconsciously saving for the day that... well, when something like this happened. Now I've got the money to bring this old place back to life."

The other man whistled. "You're either really dedicated to your grandpa, or your job was utter hell. That's the only reason I can think of that would make someone wanna come out here and work on a farm by themselves."

"Worse than hell, actually... insurance." Dean snorted at Mikael's grimace. "Yeah, that's about what I thought, too, and then some. I was going to school to do this sort of thing before I had to change, though. So it isn't like I hadn't thought about it before."

"What made you change your mind?"

Even after all these years, the question still caused an empty feeling in Dean's chest. It wasn't nearly as bad as it had once been, time had eased some of the pain. However, he didn't think you ever really moved on from losing family like that.

"Life got in the way. It has a way of doing that," Dean said. "Had to change plans if I wanted to eat... which is kind of ironic when you think about it."

"Turning away from farming so you can afford to eat?

Yeah, just a bit. But hey, now you got the place, the money, and the college education. That's something, right?"

Dean couldn't help smiling. There was no mocking of his education in the man's voice. Dean wasn't necessarily ashamed of the education he'd received. He knew how some people could be about that sort of thing, particularly when it came to farming, his grandfather included. People tended to regard learning about it in a classroom as almost cheating, faking, or unnecessary, and not nearly as practical as living it and learning on the job. Dean was pretty sure the only reason he'd been spared any scorn so far was because of his grandfather's reputation. That, and those who had welcomed him had been those who'd known him when he was a child. At least they knew he wasn't a stranger to the hard work that went into a farm.

"I'm still amazed that he left all of this to me," he said. "I'm just... trying to do what's right by him and the farm."

Mikael's head cocked again and he nodded slowly. "I understand. But don't worry. The whole town's talking about what you're doing. Everyone says that your grandpa would be very proud of you. I can't argue with it, and hey, it's giving me work, too."

Dean chuckled, warming up to the man even more. "I appreciate that, and I hope it's true."

A crash sounded, causing them both to snap their heads up at a sudden movement. Jax stood in the dining room window, his whole body wriggling as he gazed at them with longing.

Dean sighed. "Meet my little ox."

"Aw, he's sweet. Hey, buddy!" Mikael waved at the dog, who wriggled even more fiercely in the window and barked. "Alright, I should probably get moving. I don't have a phone so if you need to get ahold of me before tomorrow just give

Old Man Wright a call. Otherwise I'll be back to get started on the shed first thing in the morning."

Dean shook Mikael's hand, liking the warmth and strength of his grip. It was only polite to casually watch as the man walked back to his truck. Now, there was a man who knew how to fill out a pair of slightly dirty jeans just right. Making sure he wasn't caught ogling, Dean turned back toward the house.

He could only sigh to himself. One day, and he was already admiring the assets of the very nice and most likely straight carpenter sent to work on his property. Maybe he should have tried to have a bit of fun before leaving the city. Out here, it would be harder to scratch that itch, especially with everything he had to get done. Well, it had never been much of a priority before, and he wasn't about to make it one now.

Mikael honked and waved as he turned around and drove down the path back to the road. Dean waved before walking into the house. Mikael had been the first person his age he'd met whose face he hadn't recognized from his youth. Then again, the heater guy probably fit that bill as well, but Dean couldn't even remember his name. It seemed almost a good omen, to find something new among the familiar.

3

*I*n many ways, he was happy he'd chosen to do all the work before spring had fully arrived. The temperature swung wildly back and forth, depending on the day. It had eventually stayed warm enough for the ground to thaw so he would be able to work the fields. It still remained cool, though, so he was able to labor throughout the day without feeling like he was going to drop.

The work of cleaning the entire house was finished, and the unpacking was coming along at a decent pace. However, he would have to start work on the rest of the property if he wanted to have anything growing and harvested by the end of the season. That meant ordering seeds and fertilizer. Again, he found himself indebted to Davis. The lawyer had managed to get him a list of suppliers with some good deals thrown in before he'd even finished breakfast on the same morning he called.

The order would arrive in a few days, which meant there was time enough for him to clear the fields. That was easier said than done. The rich earth that had been tilled dutifully every year was now buried beneath a sea of wild grass and assorted weeds. The first day Mikael came to work on the property was the day Dean decided to devote his time to reclaiming the fields from the wild.

Mikael showed up first thing in the morning as planned, with a wide grin for Dean when he spotted him. "G'morning!" the carpenter said.

Dean hadn't been awake long. He did have coffee, however, which he needed before doing much of anything in the morning. Managing a weak smile, he greeted Mikael and told him to help himself to anything in the kitchen, particularly the fridge.

"Got more food than you know what to do with, eh?" Mikael grinned knowingly, shading his eyes against the rising sun as he assessed Dean. "You alright?"

Dean snorted. "Yeah, just never been a morning person. I'd offer you coffee, but you don't look like you need it."

"Naw, don't need it much, but I like it now and again."

"Well, feel free to help yourself to it, and yeah, there's more food there than I'm going to be able to eat in the next month, so you can help yourself to that, too."

"Wait until you start working out in the fields—you'll eat more than you think. By the end of the week, you'll be eating like you were fourteen again. Trust me." Mikael laughed, patting Dean's shoulder and turning back to the truck to get his equipment. Dean warmed slightly at the touch. Mikael getting more than a handful of words out of him this early in the morning was a feat in itself.

Dean dragged himself out into the fields to begin his own work. Even with access to his grandfather's modern equipment, Dean spent most of the first day clearing an area of the vegetation. He needed the wild grass short enough that when he did eventually till the ground, he wouldn't risk the equipment seizing up from the tangled grass. Fortunately, he'd gotten to it before the growing season started. Although the equipment made more than enough noise to block out nearly everything else, he caught glances of Mikael now and again. The sound of hammering rang in the air, and for just a moment, Dean thought he heard singing as well. Mikael's call alerted him to the time.

Mikael hadn't taken him up on the offer of coffee, but he willingly took up the offer of food. Apparently, the casseroles and pies that stuffed Dean's fridge were far more appetizing than whatever the man had brought with him. Somewhat shockingly, Mikael had already helped himself to an entire casserole dish before Dean joined him to tuck into another one. Later, the two of them quietly enjoyed some apple pie while lazing in the warming afternoon sun. Already, Dean was feeling the effects of the physical work clearing the fields, knowing that by the end of the week it would be a miracle if he could move his body at all.

"So, what brought you out here?" Mikael asked as they finished their slices of pie. "I mean, besides the farm. What made you wanna drop everything and come and run it?"

Dean shrugged and was slow to answer. "I guess it was just time for a change. Like I told you, I always wanted to do this, even as a kid. I guess when I was given the opportunity, I couldn't pass it up. It seemed like the right choice at the time."

"Must be one helluva passion for you to drop all that city life in exchange for living here. Leaving your life behind like that, everyone you ever really knew, all to come slave away in the dirt and mud."

"Felt right. Wasn't really leaving anyone behind, either, so there wasn't much holding me back, other than just taking the risk."

"You didn't have any friends or family?"

Dean's gaze shifted away from Mikael to watch Jax instead. The dog had woken from his afternoon nap and was occupying himself by attempting to catch every small creature that came within range. Dean was pretty sure the dog wasn't going to catch anything, since the dopey animal barked as loudly as he could whenever he spotted something moving. Everything was well warned of Jax's approach before he even thought about charging after it.

"The only family I ever had was my parents and my Grandpa," Dean said. "My mom and dad died about a year before Grandpa. Didn't have anyone else but them. Honestly, never really had many friends either. I've had a few here and there, but it just never really worked out I guess. I've never been a particularly social person."

He sounded almost casual, as if he didn't know the exact date of each death and as if he hadn't cared about not having a relationship. To Mikael's credit, at least in Dean's mind, the man looked neither uncomfortable nor pitying. Dean was thankful that he hadn't even brought up sympathy for his loss. The one thing that Dean had quickly grown tired of were the condolences. That, and the people who seemed compelled to keep him company when he kept to himself afterward. The idea of having friends who were there only out of pity left a bad taste in his mouth.

"Nobody special?" Mikael asked, the casual curiosity obvious in his voice.

Dean had to laugh at that. "No, nobody special. Wasn't really the dating type, either."

"Never got lonely?"

Dean raised a brow. "Are you asking what I think you're asking?"

It was Mikael's turn to laugh. "Maybe a little, but I meant *actually* lonely. Not 'go out and get laid' lonely."

"I guess. You get so used to being by yourself and doing your own thing for so long, it just becomes normal. Sometimes I missed having other people around, but I think my job had me spending more time dealing with people than I liked. Besides, I have these crazy guys to look after."

Dean nodded toward Jax darting across the yard and to Nix, who had quietly emerged from somewhere in the house to find a perch on the window sill. Mikael grinned, and Dean could hear the laughter in his voice, "Okay, and the other lonely?"

Dean rolled his eyes, trying to ignore the man's probing. "That's what bar visits were for."

"Huh, maybe you have a better grasp on living than most people." Mikael laughed again but he sounded serious when he said it. He got up, saying he needed to get back to work. Dean watched him walk back to the equipment shed, realizing he hadn't had the chance to ask Mikael much of anything.

Only later did he realize that Mikael had asked if Dean had *anybody* special. Not girlfriend, or wife, but "someone special." Did Mikael know somehow? His grandfather had known about Dean's sexual and romantic inclination, of course. Grandpa had been the first person he'd told. The old man was certainly the salt-of-the earth type, traditional, and Old World in so many ways. Yet, when the young Dean had come to him, trembling all over, and told the man his dreaded secret, his Grandpa's reaction had been to wrap the teenager up in a hug. Dean never quite knew what his grandfather truly thought about his disclosure, except that he'd been adamant that Dean was who he was and that his grandfather loved him and just wanted him to be happy.

That revelation had happened during one of the last summers he'd spent here, and he hadn't told anyone else in the area. He knew his grandfather wouldn't have passed that little tidbit on. As far as his grandfather was concerned, it was no one's business but Dean's. Since Dean was more often mistaken for straight, he wondered if Mikael was simply being polite. It wouldn't be too far-fetched to think that some of the neutral, politically correct ideals of urban social circles had leaked into the countryside. Mikael was certainly of an age that he might have picked some of that up.

He was over-thinking things again. What Mikael had said could have been an indicator that the man knew or suspected, or it might have simply been a turn of phrase and he had meant nothing by it at all. Dean wouldn't deny that a part of him wondered if that meant he wasn't alone out here, after all. It wasn't as if gay people weren't born and raised out in the middle of nowhere, too. But he had always doubted his chances of finding someone like him out here, especially someone who looked as good as Mikael.

Finally he managed to shake those thoughts out of his head as he immersed himself in his work. The mindless but intensive labor had been enough to clear his head, and by the time he had finished his work, the sun was beginning to set. When he dragged himself back toward the house, he found Mikael loading his tools up. Dean hadn't even thought to notice the progress on the shed as he went by, and there was no way he was going to go stomping back to find out, either. Mikael had been right about the day's work exhausting him—nothing sounded better at the moment than collapsing into bed.

"Looks like you need to go crack open a cold one," Mikael noted, amused.

Dean managed to crack a weary smile. "Ugh, I wish. Didn't get the chance to get any before my fridge got stuffed to the gills with all that food. Gonna have to eat out some space first."

Mikael seemed almost horrified. "You don't have any beer?"

Dean laughed. "Nope, wasn't high on the list of priorities at the time."

"Sheesh. Don't you know how it works? Coffee in the morning, lemonade or tea in the afternoon, and a beer to watch the sun set. Trust me, nothing is better after a long, hard day than to sit and watch the sun setting with a beer in your hand."

"I'll keep that in mind," Dean said, thinking he might have to try that one day. If only to find out what the hype was all about.

"Good, you do that."

Mikael jumped into his truck. Dean stood there for a moment, returning his wave before retreating into the house. Once he was indoors, hunger overwhelmed his desire to lie down and Dean found himself thankful that his fridge was stuffed with food as he heated himself up a full meal. Mikael hadn't been wrong when he'd talked about his appetite after a long day of work. Dean had inhaled the food as if he'd been starved for days, then retired to the living room.

It was a short evening, but he managed to pull a few more things out of the boxes. It was neat to see what he would find, and then decide where each item should go. There were strange pieces of a wood sculpture that wasn't familiar to him and a necklace made entirely of silver. The pendant on it was small, and it took Dean a moment to decipher what was engraved on it. In the circle of silver lay etched an Old World depiction of a wolf, its features harsher and more demonic than he would have expected. He recog-

nized it, however. It was the necklace he had seen his grandfather wearing now and again.

After setting aside the sculpture and the pendant, only a
stubborn force of will kept him going for a couple more
hours before he decided to give up the fight. He, along with
Jax and Nix, all retreated upstairs to his bedroom. It was
customary for him to read for a while before going to sleep
and both dog and cat would curl up with him on the bed
while he relaxed. Tonight, though, he found his eyes drifting
closed after only a few pages. Giving up the struggle he
rolled over, falling asleep almost instantly.

His dreams were peculiar—and a little unnerving.
When he woke up the next morning, he could vaguely
remember the sensation of walking on all fours through a
moonlit forest. It had felt odd but he easily shook it off as he
padded down to the kitchen to make himself a much-
needed pot of coffee. His body had all the aches he had
been expecting, and he suspected it was only going to get
worse. As tempted as he was to spend the day relaxing and
allowing his body to recover a bit, he had no time for that.

Mikael showed up right around the same time as the day
before, this time accepting the coffee Dean offered him.
There wasn't much chatting that morning, for which Dean
was grateful. It was tempting to say that all the time he'd
spent alone had caused his slow morning routine to become
more of an addiction. Yet, even as a kid he'd been terrible
about waking up. It wasn't that he was necessarily a night
owl either, though he could stay up late if need be. Mornings had always been a slow push to wakefulness, no matter
how much he'd tried to change it.

The next task he had to deal with was removing the
rocks from the long stretches of now- rimmed fields. He
couldn't till the land with large rocks still on the ground. He

might have had plenty of money to get himself started on the farm, but he wasn't exactly eager to spending so much of it on replacing any large equipment. He already knew that he was going to be leaning heavily on his savings with all the work still ahead of him.

Removing the rocks had taken the better part of the day, then dragged on well into the next day before he was finally satisfied that he wouldn't break anything when he tilled the field. He also had himself a nice big pile of rocks that he wasn't quite sure what to do with.

After the time spent breaking his back to clear the fields, Dean was thankful that his grandfather had invested in modern equipment and hadn't been so old fashioned as to require a horse-drawn plow. Luckily, the tractor worked just fine with the right attachment, and it proved a far less strenuous task than the previous few days of manual labor had been. The monotony was less enjoyable, however. After a couple of passes learning how to maneuver the machinery, Dean could practically switch to autopilot. He occupied himself by watching Mikael's progress as he worked his way through the various repairs on the property.

The irrigation system was Dean's next project. It was far easier said than done, however. Mikael had even paused in his own work long enough to wander over and chuckle at Dean's frustration before actually relenting and helping him. Dean had grumbled and griped, but he'd allowed it, and secretly he was pleased at Mikael's interest in what he was doing. Thanks to his help Dean was able to get the system going just before the sky darkened.

By the time his order of seeds had shown up, Dean had been a bit surprised to find that he was ready to plant themt. He soon found out that sowing seeds was about as tedious as tilling soil. He was also aware that the entire process would lengthen as time went on. There were still a vast amount of land that he hadn't touched. Although he had certainly tackled more ground than another beginner might have, he was confident that between the education he'd received, both at school and from his grandfather, he would be able to handle it. As he gained more experience, he would rework more fields and expand his usable farmland.

Dean barely had the chance to feel proud of himself before he spotted Mikael sitting on the steps of the porch. Mikael was watching him as he approached, and for just a second, Dean felt the urge to flee like a startled deer. For the briefest of moments, Dean felt a strange sensation that something predatory and deadly was watching his approach. The appearance of the man's sudden grin set him at ease and wiped the strange thought from his mind. Mikael then held out a brown glass bottle.

"No way!" Dean exclaimed, reaching out to take it. "Where'd the beer come from?"

"Brought it with me in my cooler. You didn't seem to be getting any, so I figured I should." He lifted a brow and, opening his beer, took a long drink from it.

Dean hesitated before Mikael scooted over, making room on the step next to him. Taking the offer, he sat down and opened his own beer. To his surprise, the beer was ice cold and tasted delicious as it slid down his throat. The noise he made bordered on pornographic as he took another drink, savoring the taste.

"Told ya," Mikael snickered.

"Thank you so much," Dean moaned. He knew that beer had a tendency to taste good at the most random of times. It occurred to him that the taste had a lot to do with the mood he was in. The sheer satisfaction of a long list of tasks completed, successfully moving him along the path he had chosen, put him in one of those moods. He looked at the common brand of beer in his hand. "Wow. I'd have sworn this was some special brew."

"Nope, that's just a job well done and a sunset to enjoy. You can rest a little now, my friend." Mikael grinned, saluting Dean with his bottle.

"Not for long. Sure, I don't have to fret over the fields too much now, but the rest of this place still really needs to be touched up. I eventually have to get some animals in here too, once those buildings are ready. Then I have to make sure I have everything I need for them while making sure I don't plummet myself into bankruptcy in the process."

"Hey." Mikael motioned to the horizon with the hand holding tight to his bottle. "Ignore all that for a minute and look at that instead."

Dean followed the direction of the man's hand, obeying his command to basically shut up. The sky seemed to be slowly burning as the sun set. Red, orange, and yellow— each hue a different intensity that stretched across the sky. The clouds seemed to glow with it, burning along with the rest of the sky. The faint wind rustled the trees, carrying the sounds of the emerging insects and frogs to their ears. It was far more beautiful than he had appreciated only moments ago.

A small sound escaped him as he leaned back against the top step, beer loose in his hand as he sipped at it. Neither man spoke as the sun continued its journey out of sight. Nothing broke the moment as the sky began to darken, the fiery colours fading away. The purple of twilight began to take over, and it would be a while before the pure blackness of night sank in. Night time here was... well, dark. If you didn't have a light handy when you were outside after dark, you couldn't see your hand in front of your face.

Dean glanced over at Mikael as the last of the light dwindled away. He was a little startled to find the man already looking at him, and it seemed like maybe he had been for a while. Dean blinked slowly, forgetting what he was about to say. The low light, left behind by the setting sun, cast shadows over Mikael's face, making it seem almost as menacing as it was beautiful. That ominous edge enhanced it, somehow.

He couldn't tell if the moment had actually stretched on for as long as it seemed. He sensed something emanating from Mikael, something he could almost put a name to. The shadows added an intensity to the look on Mikael's face, but Dean would swear that the man was considering closing the distance between them. Perhaps he was only seeing what he wanted to, but it didn't make the feeling any less exhilarating.

"So," Mikael said, breaking the illusion of danger with the flash of a cocky smile, "what'd you think?"

Dean nodded slowly. "Thank you, Mikael. I needed that. I'm so caught up in the details of getting everything done that I guess I forget why I wanted to do this in the first place. Grandpa always said I thought too much about everything."

"Maybe it's just that you're thinking the wrong way. Sometimes you just have to... let things happen. Go with what is and let the rest sort itself out."

"Not really my expertise," he admitted.

Dean had never been very good at giving up control, if he were honest with himself. Long before everything had gone to hell and he'd changed his whole life around, he'd already been like that. He was never content just to let things happen; he was always determined to make them happen, and make them happen in just the way he wanted them to. If he couldn't force things to go his way, he at least tried to predict what would happen so he could prepare. He would take a situation, turn it in every direction and dissect it carefully, a little anxiously, looking at it from every angle. It wasn't in a slow, methodical way, either. It was often done with a hasty anxiety that bordered on a complete freak-out.

But he admired Mikael's attitude. He might never have been able to pull it off himself, but he could certainly appreciate someone else being able to. He had to admit he envied him a little, as well. People like Mikael always seemed to radiate a calm aura. That "whatever happens, happens" attitude seemed to bring a peace to their lives that was palpable.

Even Mikael couldn't deny it. "Yeah, you are a bit antsy. That's alright though. People like you get stuff done. You're not afraid to stick your neck out. Dunno if I could have ever done what you did; pack up my life and move it somewhere where everything was completely different."

Dean was a little taken aback by the compliment. "It wasn't that big a deal. Plus, from what I can see, working outside of The Grove isn't exactly normal. I'm betting you took your own risks with that, even if it's just because of some of the town's attitude to all of you."

That seemed to give the other man pause. The encroaching darkness made his facial expression hard to read and Dean was a little afraid that he'd said something wrong.

"Heh, guess you have a point there," Mikael finally conceded. His tone was off, though it still had a playful swagger to it. "My one little rebellion. Still doesn't hold a candle to what you did, but we can agree to disagree."

Dean wanted to ask what the man had meant by 'rebellion.' Sure, it was probably a big thing to step outside of one's community like that, especially one as insular as The

Grove. It was the phrasing of it that had Dean's brow cocking, though Mikael either didn't notice or chose to ignore it. Before Dean could ask for clarification, the taller man was pushing himself up from the step with a groan.

"Alright, I should probably head out. I won't be able to get back out here 'til Monday. Got some family stuff to deal with through the rest of the weekend. Don't worry, I'll be back bright and early Monday morning."

"Sure, that's fine. I'm probably going to lay off a bit this weekend, anyway."

Mikael stood up and headed towards his truck. "Good. You deserve it. Maybe take one of your neighbors up on their invitations. I hear the people out here make a mean dinner for company." Dean didn't have to see the man to hear the familiar grin on his face. "Take it easy, Dean."

"G'night, Mikael," he called out.

Dean mulled over the conversation as the truck roared to life and pulled out. True, he'd only known the man a handful of days, yet they'd gotten to know each other pretty well in that short time. Mikael hadn't been averse to taking a break with Dean now and then to just talk, though only occasionally did they stray near anything personal or serious. All the same, he had learned a little bit about the man, especially where his behavior was concerned.

One thing Dean could say about being a loner was that he was good at reading people. He had developed the trait on an intuitive level, and his instincts were almost always completely accurate.

Mikael struck him as genuine and trustworthy right from their first conversation, though he could be a little evasive and even secretive. Dean could respect the man's privacy, and he hadn't wanted to pry too much, despite his curiosity. Yet, the past couple of days, Mikael had seemed a little off. There appeared to be more restless energy rolling off him. It skewed the laidback attitude he'd exhibited the first few days. Dean seriously hoped that the 'family stuff' he'd mentioned wasn't the cause, but the energy had seemed almost anxious. Dean wondered if there was perhaps some friction in the family.

Knowing he wasn't going to get any answers by obsessing over it, he decided to continue following Mikael's advice. He leaned back on the top step again, letting his body relax. Jax joined him, padding out of the darkness to sit next to his best friend. Dean wrapped a companionable arm around the dog, hugging him close. The two of them watched together as one by one the stars came to life in the immense black sky. Then they watched the full, bright moon rise up from the horizon before eventually returning to the house for some well-earned sleep.

4

---

*O*n Sunday Dean called the Williams's house to accept the dinner offer, if it still stood. Mrs. Williams was positively overjoyed at the idea and thanked him for calling early in the day so she could prepare for his visit. He tried to tell her not to go to any trouble, but the older woman promptly told him to never mind and to be there at five o'clock sharp.

"I know it's a bit late for supper, but that's the way Earl likes it. I hope that isn't a problem," she said, sounding a little worried.

Dean thought about all the times he hadn't eaten dinner till almost ten o'clock or later and chuckled. "No, Mrs. Williams, that sounds perfect. I'll see you at five then."

He eyed the couch longingly and contemplated lying back down. Ever since Friday, when he'd told Mikael he was going to rest up and take it easy for the weekend, the couch had become his best friend. He really wanted to put something beneath the large window facing out to the front of the house, though. As it was, he'd spent a good chunk of time sprawled on the couch, facing that same window. It had been relaxing to lay there for a while, book in hand, enjoying the scenery whenever he glanced up.

There was no such a thing as a real day off when managing a farm. He'd checked the fields to make sure the watering system was working properly. He still had boxes to unpack, as well, even though he'd nearly finished and everything was just about ready to use. What was left was the little details that would make the house a home, mostly dragging out pictures, paintings, and various knick-knacks. Eventually, he would have to set up the other two bedrooms. Though he wasn't expecting to have guests staying, it would help to complete the picture.

Going into Sunday, he had allowed himself to sleep an extra couple of hours before finally forcing himself from the warm comfort of his bed. In truth, once he was awake and pushing himself to get to work, the feeling of comfort remained. He still wasn't sure that all this change was leading anywhere good, but he couldn't help the gut feeling that this was exactly where he belonged.

After his call to Mrs. Williams, he successfully fought the urge to fall back onto the couch, instead he tackled the remaining stack of boxes. It had been a bit tricky to take bits from his boxes and combine them with his grandfather's things to create a cohesive collection. He was conscious that old and new could often clash. He was trying to create an atmosphere in the house that spoke both of its history and of himself. He was having fun giving the place a makeover and trying to bring the two together in a way that made sense, all the while making quiet jokes at his own expense.

The relaxing day passed quickly but eventually it was time to jump in the shower and change into more presentable clothes. Once upon a time he'd preferred to shower in the morning, to help wake him up. Since coming to the farm, that was another thing that had changed. He couldn't very well sleep in his bed covered in the sweat and grime of the day.

Dean stood on the Williams' porch, knocking on the door, a good fifteen minutes early. Mrs. Williams quickly let him in, immediately making a fuss over him. He hadn't been in the house very often when he was younger—his child-hood in the area had been spent mostly outdoors. Yet, from what he could remember, it didn't seem much different. It was what you'd expect a farmhouse to look like inside: old-fashioned but cozy. It felt comfortable, and he hoped that when he was done settling in, his house would make visitors feel the same way.

A cup of coffee was quickly placed in his hand, as Mrs. Williams told him to sit and make himself at home. He was all but shoved into a plush armchair that threatened to swallow him whole as he sank into it. Smiling brightly, the older woman disappeared, saying that she was off to fetch her husband. A moment later he heard the woman yelling out the back door for Mr. Williams, and Dean could only chuckle as he heard them bickering back and forth. More accurately, he could hear Mrs. Williams badgering her husband, while Mr. Williams was a faint, but deep voice in the distance.

He remembered these two had been just like that even when he was a kid. It had been unnerving at first. He'd never seen his parents engage in that type of banter, and at first he had thought Mr. and Mrs. Williams were really argu-ing. It wasn't until he was a bit older, and his grandfather had explained, that he realized the arguing was simply the way the Williams' showed each other affection. If you watched carefully when they started grousing, and caught them just at the right time, you could see the humor reflected in their eyes. Once you understood, it was nearly impossible to miss the shared warmth between them, that was something he appreciated, and also envied slightly.

"Oh, that man," she had huffed as she walked back into the room with a plate of cookies for Dean. She disappeared back to the kitchen and as much as he wished that she wouldn't go to so much trouble on his account, he wasn't going to say no to her cookies. They were still warm, probably taken from the oven only moments before he arrived. Without hesitation, he snatched one up. One bite of the cookie reminded him why he'd been so obsessed with them when he was younger.

A smile crossed his face as he heard Mr. Williams come into the house through the back door. The sound of Mrs. Williams fussing around in the kitchen now melded with their low conversation. The playful tone of their voices told Dean they were still bickering.

Mr. Williams had just finished cleaning up for dinner when Dean was summoned into the dining room. The large table was loaded with a myriad of foods that spread from one end to the other. Dean took the seat Mrs Williams offered. He was impressed, certainly flattered and maybe a little embarrassed, at the vast array of food that lay before him. She really hadn't needed to go to all that trouble on his account. The large chicken would have been plenty, let alone everything else. Mashed potatoes with steaming puddles of butter sat beside a large green bean casserole that he was pretty sure had no ingredients from a can or a box. Homemade biscuits were piled up next to a bowl of corn that he really hoped hadn't been shucked and shaved by hand. Everything here had either been grown on the property and preserved, or grown nearby. Even the jam, butter, and milk came from the farm. Save for the salt, this was about as close to the food going straight from farm to table as one could get.

Dean chuckled at the thought, drawing a questioning glance from his hosts as they seated themselves at the table. He waved it off with a smile, letting them chalk it up to whatever they wanted. He really didn't want to get into the whole obsession some city people had about farm to table. They had no real idea if their food truly came from anywhere nearby. This would have been absolute heaven to them in so many ways, yet without their locally grown, organic quinoa, they would have been absolutely miserable.

Clamping down on his reaction, he bowed his head, knowing that grace would be next. It had been years since he'd done any such thing. His faith was private, as it had been with his family when he was young. It had waned to next to nothing over the years, evaporating almost completely after the compounded loss he had endured. He had been assured by others that this was normal, and that in time his faith would return, but it hadn't. Not that Mr. and Mrs. Williams needed to know that—it was part of his private world. It was enough that he even remembered the old prayer his grandfather had always spoken at the table, reciting it perfectly now when he was asked to say the blessing.

"Bless this, the bounty of the earth that we are granted. Bless this land that provides for us all. Bless our loved ones, who bear us through the hard times. Bless our lives with plenty and love, as it is above, so it is below, thanks to the Almighty, amen."

His hosts both echoed his "amen" with one of their own before moving to dish out the food. Dean hadn't missed the curious glance Mrs. Williams shot his way when he finished giving the blessing. He'd always thought it was a strange prayer but had never thought to question it. His grandfather explained that it was an old prayer, adapted over time from the words of early inhabitants. After settlers had moved in and merged their blood with that of the native people, the words and meaning had become diluted. He supposed that made sense—the prayer didn't sound totally Christian after all—but it did the job.

They dug into the meal with gusto; the conversation sparse at first. His appetite had grown considerably since he'd returned and begun working so hard. Even when he'd been regularly working out at the gym near his apartment, he hadn't been this hungry. Now, it seemed like he couldn't get enough food. Even at breakfast, which used to be when he was least hungry, he was eating more food than ever before.

The meal was excellent, so that probably had a lot to do with it. It seemed Mrs. Williams was a whiz in the kitchen. Her skills weren't limited to baking cookies and pies—everything had been fresh and delicious. Despite how much he was enjoying the main course, he definitely looked forward to dessert. Though her culinary talents were obviously broad, they were at their very best where desserts were concerned.

After they'd properly settled down to the meal, they began to talk a little morel. Mr. and Mrs. Williams were curious to learn about everything he'd been up to in the last few years. Except for his grandfather's funeral, they hadn't seen him since he was a teenager, so there was plenty to tell. While he wasn't normally one for sharing personal details, he couldn't begrudge them wanting to know more, particularly Mrs. Williams. It only seemed natural for them to wonder what he'd been up to since they last saw him.

He explained about college and briefly touched on why

he had made the change after his parents had died. He smiled when Mrs. Williams nodded solemnly, and reached for his hand across the table.

Not for the first time, he found himself glossing over the specifics of his life. He didn't share that he really hadn't been one for socializing, especially during his working years. He found it amusing that he kept that information, along with his awful love life, from other people, and yet he had shared it so readily with Mikael. Then again, he was also holding back the fact that his love life had consisted of absolutely no women... zero. That detail he hadn't told anyone, including Mikael.

"Well, I for one am happy as can be that you're back here and bringing the old place back up to scratch," Mrs. Williams said, heaping another serving of green bean casserole onto Dean's plate. "It'll be a blessing to see everything all fixed up and clean again."

"Well, it's mostly clean," Dean said, "but I've gotten some help with fixing things. Never been really good at carpentry myself."

Mr. Williams looked up from his plate. "I heard Clint sent someone over to work on the place. Not sure he told me who, though. But the man doesn't employ anyone who doesn't know what they're doing."

"Yeah, Mikael seems to know exactly what he's doing."

"Mikael? That the one from The Grove?"

That caught his wife's attention, her eyes darting between her husband and Dean. Dean answered cautiously, "Yeah, he said something about that."

"I never met the man," Mr. Williams admitted. "Heard he's a hard worker, though."

"Hasn't slacked yet," Dean replied with a smile. He couldn't even picture Mikael slacking. The man was hard-working and driven, from what he could tell. He certainly knew when to take a break, but he wasn't the type to lie around longer than necessary. In the short time Dean had gotten to know the man, he seemed like the type to both work hard and play hard.

"Asking for trouble, having him over there, if you ask me," Mrs. Williams said. Dean was startled to hear the distaste in her voice that bordered on disgust. The woman's normally pleasant face soured as she looked from her husband to Dean. He was surprised that Mrs. Williams, of all people, was one of those who disliked residents of The Grove so intensely.

"I... why? He hasn't done anything wrong."

"He might be alright, at least at first. Would have to be if Clint was willing to take him on. But you listen to me, Dean Matthews. There ain't no one came from The Grove who wasn't trouble at some point." She huffed slightly, glowering down at her plate and pushing the food around with her fork.

"I... I don't understand. What's so bad about people from The Grove? They're just another community from around here, aren't they?" In all honesty, he really didn't understand it. He had chalked it up to a simple dislike of those that were different. That sort of attitude was uncomfortably common in small rural areas like this and was one of the biggest reasons he kept his business to himself and planned to continue that way.

"They just aren't right—never have been, even in my grandmother's time. They've been living out in those woods forever, and they don't like other people going back there, either. Your grandpa might have been able to go out there and be alright, but... weird things happen around there. You listen long enough and you don't wonder if there ain't something unnatural going on. Matter of fact, I'm sure of it. Ain't no one who come outta there who hasn't been a bit queer, Dean. They're an odd bunch, and they're always bringing trouble to this town."

"I don't think Mikael is like that at all," Dean said, trying to sound firm, but feeling a little put off by her vehemence. "He couldn't be too bad if someone from town was willing to hire him, right?"

"Clint is a good man, and he's got a good feel for how hard someone is willing to work." While it seemed like it was an agreement, Dean could hear in her voice that it was anything but. "But Clint—he ain't the best at figuring anything else out about people. If he was, he wouldn't have no one from that place working for him."

"Mikael hasn't done anything wrong, certainly not to me. He seems like a good man," Dean protested, feeling a bit defensive on the man's behalf. "He works hard, he knows what he's doing, and he feels like good people to me."

"Seems like Clint ain't the only one who ain't the best at judging people, if now you're befriending that man, Dean." Her eyes looked like they were trying to drill through Dean. Her gaze was piercing and filled with judgment. He was torn between annoyance at the sudden accusation that shouldn't even have been made in the first place, and feeling uncomfortable under her scrutiny.

"Enough, Molly," Mr. Williams said, his own eyes on Dean. "He's a grown man, not a boy anymore."

Mrs. Williams turned her attention to her husband. "You know full well what I'm talking about, Earl."

"What we say ain't gonna make a bit of difference. We gotta let the man do what he's gonna do and decide for himself. Now, don't you have a pie you wanted to show off to him?"

Mrs. Williams definitely seemed as if she had more to say on the matter. She paused, though, obviously fighting an inner battle over whether to carry on speaking. Dean hoped that she would leave well enough alone. He understood that this sort of bias wasn't uncommon out here and that it could come from the most unexpected sources. But he didn't want to entertain it any longer than he had to. As much as he wanted to dismiss her concerns, the idea of "queer" things happening out there had him wondering. He knew she'd used the word meaning "odd," but now he was curious just what sort of odd things she'd heard of.

She seemed to take the hint, though not without another meaningful look in Dean's direction as she pushed herself up from the table. Mr. Williams sat with Dean in an awkward silence, the sound of Mrs. Williams moving about in the kitchen, the only background noise.

He was relieved when Mrs. Williams returned, her usual smile back on her face as she set the chocolate cream pie down before them. Dean's mouth watered as he eyed the dessert. "Oh Lord, you remembered my favorite, didn't you?"

"The woman's got a mind like a steel trap, Dean. You can bet she remembers everything," Mr. Williams said with a slight smirk. That smirk told Dean everything he needed to know about her memory. There was no doubt that the woman probably remembered every detail and had no problem reminding others whenever she felt it necessary. He only hoped he wouldn't have to be on the receiving end again, though it was obvious it was a regular occurrence for Mr Williams.

"Hush you," she huffed, swatting her husband with a towel. "It would be hard to forget such a thing, anyway. You might have been a pretty quiet kid, Dean, but there was no hiding your love of this pie, especially since you'd eat it all if you got the chance."

Dean blushed a little, much to their amusement. He couldn't argue with the facts. If there was one thing in the world of sweets that he loved above all else, it was chocolate. What this woman could do when she threw it into a pie was nothing short of a miracle. Thankfully, he'd grown more patient as an adult, but he still found it irresistible. Though he wasn't any less greedy about it, happily accepting slice after slice that was offered to him.

He was relieved that the rest of the conversation that evening was far more relaxed and enjoyable. The Williamses shared tales about the town, and they reminisced, Mrs. Williams' eyes tearing up at one point when speaking about his grandfather. It was touching to see how well-loved he was by the people who lived here. His grandfather had been a good man, and Dean was happy to be surrounded by the people that had shared his life.

Mrs. Williams had attempted to load Dean up with even more food before he went home, right up until her husband said, "The man's gonna need a suitcase to carry all that, Molly. Might be best to take it over tomorrow."

She fussed over Dean as he left until he reassured her that there was still plenty of food left in his fridge from all the welcome visits. That seemed to mollify her enough for her to let him leave without further fretting. He happily accepted a tight hug from Mrs. Williams and a warm handshake from Mr. Williams, then stepped out into the night air.

The night was cool, but alive with the twinkling stars and the heavy, full moon. This being the last night to see it so full and bright for another month, Dean was glad it was there as he walked home.

Other than the tense moment about Mikael, he had thoroughly enjoyed his time catching up with Mr. and Mrs. Williams. If there was one thing he'd learned spending summers in this place, it was that knowing your neighbors was important. They were frequently the only company you had, especially if you lived and worked alone. The couple had always been wonderful to him as a child, and they seemed intent on being just as great now that he was back. He was glad they'd invited him over and given him the chance to experience it again.

While he knew that Mrs. Williams had meant well with her attempt to warn him, it didn't mean he wasn't still a little annoyed over it. Mikael, a man he admittedly didn't know all that well, didn't quite seem to fit the image that Mrs. Williams had presented. He couldn't be mad at her, though, and was astute enough to realize that there was probably some history there that he knew nothing about. Still, he didn't think it was fair to cast every person from The Grove in the same light, either.

His grandfather hadn't talked much about The Grove, other than to say that they were people who were simply different to the rest of us. The old man hadn't meant it as a bad thing, or that it spoke ill of the people who lived there, just that it was simply a fact. Dean could remember hearing his grandfather speak of older ways, and how the people who lived in The Grove held onto them. He never would tell Dean what those ways were, and Dean had gathered that they may not have been Christian. That was more than enough in an area like this for people to be given a bad name.

Even with those slightly troubling thoughts, it was easy enough to dismiss it as he enjoyed his walk down the moonlit road. The air was a bit too cool for him to really take his time as he would have liked, so he walked briskly pulling his jacket tightly around his shoulders. It was peaceful here though, a tranquility that he had never experienced before.

Peaceful, that is, until he heard rustling coming from the nearby woods. The sound was too heavy to be anything but a large animal. He hurried on not relishing finding out whatever had made the noise. He knew better than to run, of course. Not only would he have felt a little foolish, especially if it turned out to be nothing, but if it was a dangerous animal, he would be in worse trouble if he made a break for the house.

He heard the sound again, on his left, though not quite as heavy as before. Something much larger than a rabbit was in the woods beside him, and it seemed to be following him. In this part of the country, it could be any number of things. They weren't close enough to the mountains to seriously worry about cougars, but it was still a possibility. Coyotes, bears, and even wolves roamed these woods, which was a big reason so many locals always kept a gun handy.

He was a few feet from his gate when he heard it again, this time it was the sound of loose rocks on the road being scattered. The air was so still he could hear the soft sound of breathing, and it wasn't his own. His heart jumped into his throat and he froze in mid stride. Against his better judgement, but feeling that it was inevitable, he slowly turned. Whatever it was, he felt he needed to see what threatened him, or what was about to kill him.

A small noise escaped him when he saw the animal. An enormous wolf stood in the middle of the road, silently watching him. Television didn't do justice to the size of these animals. It might have been laughable at any other time, but not right now. The wolf was huge, it's dark fur shimmering in the moonlight. Its body seemed to ripple as it sat down, simply staring at him. He couldn't make out the animal's eyes—the shadows hid its face from view, but somehow he knew they were staring directly at him, and that mere inches from those eyes were the fanged jaws that could snap a man's bones in two with ease.

Carefully and making no abrupt moves, he took in his surroundings. The wolf didn't seem intent on attacking him, at least not at the moment. Wolves were known to be pack animals, hunting and roaming together. Where there was one, there were bound to be more. The thought that the animals were highly intelligent and were well known to use group tactics and ambushes to bring down prey made Dean break out in a cold sweat.

Seeing nothing to offer him protection and no other wolves around, he turned his attention back to the animal, who still sat watching him. Then it stood, pausing a moment to cock its head, looking almost like a harmless puppy. That innocence disappeared quickly as it took up a stalking stance and slowly began to move toward him, looking every bit like the apex predator it was. Dean fought to stay still, to keep himself from bolting and almost certainly damning himself to a painful and bloody death.

Time stood still as the wolf slowly approached. When it finally reached him, it bent its head to sniff at him, it sniffed a little here and a little there as if searching for something. Dean's heart was racing as the animal circled him, patiently pacing as it took in whatever scent it was looking for. Then it sat down and looked up at him again. From this distance, he could see the wolf's eyes better and they were much lighter than he would have guessed, though he couldn't tell the color in the moonlight. It seemed even bigger when it sat only a few inches from him, and he knew that massive body was nothing but muscle, fur, and teeth.

If he hadn't been scared out of his mind at the very thought that this animal was built to kill, he would have been in awe. Perhaps a part of him was, anyway. It was hard not to be impressed by the sight of the imposing beast. There was a beauty to it that he couldn't deny, especially since it hadn't yet bared its sharp teeth.

"Hi," he finally said in a strangled voice, surprised he hadn't been struck speechless. He was unable to think of what else to do with this strange animal.

The wolf cocked its head, sniffing him again. Dean could almost swear the animal actually understood him and this was its way of replying to his greeting. For one insane moment, he nearly reached out to pet the animal. He started to reach out, but stopped himself just in time so it only registered as a slight spasm of his arm, which, thankfully, the animal paid no attention to.

"Uh, as much as I would love to figure out why you're not trying to kill me," he said, taking a small step backward and half expecting the animal to pounce, or at least growl at the movement, "I really need to get home. Got animals of my own to feed, and I have to be up early so, if you don't mind…"

As he spoke, and silently prayed he wouldn't fall on his ass, his feet were quietly and slowly moving backwards, taking him farther and farther away. He wanted so badly to glance behind him to see where the gate was, but he didn't dare take his eyes off the wolf, who simply continued to watch him. It certainly seemed calm enough for now, giving no indication that it intended to pounce on him. But he knew better than to trust it. He had been warned many times that wolves were wily creatures.

His hands found the gate post, and he fumbled with the latch as he opened it. He vaguely remembered his grandfather warning him about the wolves around here; that they were more clever than usual. That, and to make sure not to be foolish enough to attack or try to harm them. At the time Dean had chalked it up to the fact that they were pack animals, so to attack one was to invite trouble from the others.

The wolf never stopped watching from its place on the road, and it also hadn't moved from where it sat down after its initial investigation of him. So, with the gate between them, and having put some distance between himself and the animal, he finally mustered the courage to turn around and pick up the pace. He honestly didn't know if it moved after he stopped looking at it, but so long as it didn't come after him, he didn't much care which direction it went in. Both Jax and Nix were safely tucked away in the house, and that was where he sorely wanted to be.

The house was a welcome sight as he broke through the tree line and into the open. He continually glanced over his shoulder as he walked up the drive and finally onto the porch steps. Fear told him to always keep an eye out for danger. Yet, some part of him felt the danger had passed, if it had ever been there in the first place. He knew that wolves could become used to the presence of people, but always in the context of it being a bad thing. That it made the wolves less fearful and resulted in them becoming bolder.

Even still, his breath rushed from him when the door finally closed behind him, shutting off the outside world. Calm or not, the wolf had scared the hell out of him. Sure, he'd known it was possible that some of these animals could be in the area, but it was an entirely different matter to face one down in the middle of the road at night.

How he had managed to walk away from that with nothing more than a stutter of his heart, he didn't know. Oddly enough, he hadn't ever heard of wolves behaving like that before. They typically kept their distance from people. When they weren't distant, they were either too hungry or too desperate to care, and that was bad for whoever happened to be nearby. Whatever the case, he would have to make sure to keep his animals in at night.

A loud thump from somewhere in the house made him jump and let out at yelp of fear. The source of the noise revealed itself at the end of the hallway, coming from the kitchen. He narrowed his eyes at Jax accusingly as the dog madly bounded down the hallway. Jax was so happy that he curled his body as he wagged his butt in a fit of utter joy. Dean smiled indulgently as he bent to hug and greet the dog, thinking this was about as close to a wolf as he ever wanted to get.

5

"*M*orning!" Mikael's friendly greeting caught Dean's attention from where he lounged on the front porch.

He'd decided to enjoy the morning from a comfy and relatively safe place out there. The repairs to the porch were yet to be done, but Dean knew where the sturdier points were. He'd been sitting out there for quite some time with a blanket wrapped around his shoulders against the cool of the morning, when Mikael had shown up in his truck.

"G'morning," Dean replied, trying not to sound too sleepy. He'd slept a little late this morning, so the coffee hadn't yet kicked in. Mikael seemed to notice, grinning at Dean as he dug around in his truck for his tools.

"Did I miss anything fun?" he asked, approaching the porch as he spoke.

"Mostly a lazy weekend. Went to the Williams' for dinner, though." Dean snorted, remembering the night before. "I made a friend, I think... or at least I didn't get eaten."

Mikael grinned. "A new friend? Thought you weren't big on people."

"Good thing it was a wolf, then," he shot back, equally amused at the blink he witnessed on Mikael's face.

"A wolf?" Mikael cocked his head a little. "They don't normally come down here too much. You're okay though, right?"

"Yeah, but it was by far the weirdest wolf ever," Dean replied dryly, bringing a chuckle from Mikael. "You laugh, but I'm serious. Damn thing followed me. Comes out into the road after me, and just... sniffs me. Then plops down in the middle of the road and just lets me just walk away. It didn't do anything else but watch me go. Is that normal wolf behavior to you?"

Mikael was thoughtful for a moment before shaking his head, "No, I guess that isn't too normal. Wolves around here can be kinda weird sometimes, but not usually that bizarre. Maybe he just really liked the way you smelled or something."

"Fine, but it'd be great if he'd done it in a way that didn't make me wanna pee myself."

"Be sure to tell him next time."

"Next time?" Dean raised a brow.

A wicked grin stretched across Mikael's face. "Obviously, he liked how you smelled. Maybe you'll find him curled up on your front porch one of these nights."

"Ugh, let's not do that, okay? It's too early to think about walking out to a freaking wolf on my front porch."

"At least you wouldn't need coffee to get going that morning."

"Ergh, don't you have work to do?" Dean huffed, waving the laughing man off. The very idea might have been hilarious to Mikael, but the event was still too fresh in Dean's mind. The thought of the animal even coming close to him again was less than amusing.

He watched the carpenter walk off, glancing back to Dean before continuing on with another laugh. Dean gave another huff and focused on draining the rest of his coffee. There was still plenty of work to do, even before bringing in the farm animals. He supposed that with Mikael now working on the barn, he would have to start thinking about getting a few. Eventually, he had to heave himself up from his seat and get to work making sure this place was in good condition again.

With the fields planted and growing, next on his list was to tackle the rest of the weeds. Everything around the farm had grown wild and become almost unmanageable in the past few years. There was plenty to keep him busy. He wasn't quite sure if that was a good thing or not, considering the stiffness and aches he was still experiencing from the previous week. No one else was going to do it for him, though.

He began out near the fields and the fenced in pasture, planning to work his way in. It was important to make sure that the pasture was usable for the animals that would eventually be housed there. The rest just needed to be cut back, or at least trimmed. By not just mowing it down as close as possible and tearing it all up, he made more work for himself. Not that he really wanted land that was nothing but torn up loose soil.

It took all week to return the whole area, from the fields and pasture up to the house, back to a reasonable condition. He had really wanted to landscape it a bit more, perhaps adding some plants of his own or some bushes but as good as that sounded, it would have to wait until next year. Despite having a large chunk of his savings left, he didn't want to strain his budget just in case something came up before he could start making money from everything he'd achieved so far.

Mikael had kept just as busy as he had throughout the week, though Dean had noticed the man took a few more breaks than usual. Dean wasn't about to complain, even if it did distract him from his own work whenever Mikael wandered over to talk for a bit. Like the man wasn't distracting enough but it made it even more difficult to focus on his work rather than rest his eyes on the man that looked so good in a shirt and jeans, they should have been illegal on him. When Dean was close enough, he was witness to the muscles of the man's body rolling and moving beneath his sun-touched skin.

The fact was, Mikael was almost the only company Dean had on the farm. Honestly, their time together consti-tuted the most socializing Dean had done in quite a while. The man's friendly nature helped a lot, but the fact that he respected Dean's private nature made a huge difference, as well. In truth, Dean found himself opening up to Mikael far more than he was used to. While he could be quiet, he wasn't really what you would call shy. It was just a matter of not feeling totally comfortable with other people, wari-ness that had grown worse as he'd grown older. Yet with Mikael, he found it easy to talk quite freely. Mikael's laid back and accepting manner invited him to open up and trust him.

They shared quite a bit over the course of their various conversations, whether it was during an impromptu break in the middle of the day, a brief conversation in the morn-ing, one of their talks during their shared lunch break, or the longer ones at the end of the day. Without any conscious decision they had fallen naturally into taking turns providing the beer they drank as they watched the sunset together each evening.

Conversations during the day were usually quite relaxed and playful. After hearing earlier in the week that Dean didn't care much for sports, Mikael continued to bemoan it later in the week. Dean thought it was a pity that Mikael didn't read all that much—the man claimed he could never really get into books. Both enjoyed video games, when they could find the time, not that they could settle on which game or system was best. Movies were another topic they were split on. Dean was quite open about his terrible taste in movies and Mikael sighed at the titles the smaller man rattled off during one particular lunch break.

"It's like you choose the worst movies possible, man," Mikael groaned, looking totally dejected while Dean grinned at his discomfort.

"I love bad movies because they're bad, especially if they're over-the-top action movies. Those are the best."

"Yeah, but there are good movies out there with over-the-top action, too, you know. Just let me show you a few one of these days, and maybe I can still save you from the hell you've put yourself into without even knowing it."

"Fine, if you're not busy this weekend, bring a few over and we can make a whole thing of it." Dean laughed, flicking a potato chip at him.

Mikael dodged the chip, sighing with relief. "God yes, I'll come over Saturday. You make the food—I'll bring the movies and beer."

"Pfft, I'll just go get a frozen pizza, some chips and salsa."

"Cheap date, eh? Fine, but at least make it good frozen pizza—none of that generic crap."

Dean ignored the little flutter in his chest. "Demanding, aren't you? You better put out if I'm going to have to fork out for the good stuff... Ooh! That means we can see one or two from my horror movie collection."

Mikael's groan had been all Dean needed to make him burst out laughing. The bigger man despaired at the thought of how utterly bad Dean's taste in movies was. Dean was honestly alright with that. At least he could claim that he was still enjoying what he was watching, even if he knew it was total trash.

The ease forming between them in such a short space of time was a source of comfort to Dean. For a man who had always had a hard time connecting with other people, forming such a quick bond with someone was intensely gratifying. It was a little confusing, too. The two of them seemed to fall into a relaxed, laid back pattern despite only knowing each other for a couple of weeks. Dean only had one small concern; his attraction to Mikael hadn't waned in the slightest, making him completely afraid of screwing up their friendship.

It wouldn't be an absurd idea for Dean to develop more than friendly feelings for Mikael. It was more than simple physical attraction, though he had to admit there was plenty of that to work with. The man's very nature drew Dean in— easily. Mikael was quick to laugh and play, lightening the mood with his way of teasing and joking. He could also be serious, thoughtful, and even kind. The man's compassion for Dean's life was amazing in its simplicity and in its utter lack of pity.

Perhaps it was the years spent being on his own, finally catching up to him. The promise of having a normal, relaxing day simply being around the other man was appealing—to be around someone whose company he thoroughly enjoyed and just doing... nothing. Dean hadn't had an opportunity to appreciate something like that for quite a while. He hoped the fear he felt for his budding feelings was simply an overactive imagination and his instinctive para-noia. His only consolation was that if his feelings were ever more than friendship, then he would deal with it when it was required.

If it was required.

While his fears were certainly unsettling, he found he was able to push them from his mind while focusing on his work. Between working hard and the breaks they took to get to know one another, he found he didn't have as much time for obsessing and worrying over everything. Even in the free moments when he wasn't working or caught up in conversation, he was usually too tired to do much heavy thinking. Even though he had more physical energy than before, he always seemed completely drained by the end of the day and he was as slow as ever to get started in the morning.

The rest of the week flew by. Despite the more frequent breaks Dean had taken with Mikael, his work had come along nicely. Everything from the fields and pasture up to the house had been trimmed and wrangled into submission. No longer did the vast majority of the property look as if it were one step away from becoming a wilderness. It finally looked like someone lived there and was taking care of the place again.

Saturday afternoon Dean was enjoying the fruits of his labor from his spot on the front porch. The barn was nearly done, needing only a few more tweaks and a good coat or two of paint. Mikael assured him that the building would be ready by the middle of the next week, and he could move on to the other projects on the property. With that assurance, Dean arranged for the first animals to be brought in. A few cows and goats would be enough to keep him busy, though he did add a couple more, just to make sure he wasn't being overly conservative.

It was hard to believe that he'd only been on the farm a few weeks. The sheer amount of work he'd accomplished in such a short time astounded him. Sure, the porch was still a hazard, the coops needed tending to, several things on the exterior of the house needed fixing, and Lord knew the whole thing needed to be painted. There were still open boxes lying around inside the house waiting to be unpacked but despite it all, he couldn't help but feel proud at what he'd achieved, along with an eagerness to continue making progress.

His musing was cut off by the sound of a familiar truck coming down the drive. Mikael's truck came into view, bouncing along. The truck suddenly jumped, and Dean winced, noting that perhaps the drive should be his project for the start of next week. It wouldn't really help to have things looking so much better, only to have the route to his house continue to be a hazard.

Mikael didn't seem the least bit fazed as he hopped from the cab of his truck. As promised, he had the beer and movies in hand. Dean didn't much like the fluttering in his chest as he watched the man approach, but the anticipation didn't stop the usual happy smile plastered on his face.

"Ya know," Mikael began as he climbed the stairs of the porch, "I hadn't really noticed before, but driving up here today, it's amazing how much you've gotten done. The place looks like it's loved again."

Dean squirmed a little at the compliment, squinting at the peeling paint of the house. "Well, sort of loved, anyway."

Mikael didn't miss the heaviness in Dean's voice. "Hey, come on, don't do that. You haven't been here that long and you've gotten an awful lot done, man. You need to be proud of that."

Another squirm, then a shrug. "I know, and I am... kinda. I just feel bad that this place sat here for so long and I never bothered to look into it. I let this place fall apart, even though Grandpa had left it to me. Hell, I let that damn envelope sit around forever because I was too scared to look at it."

Mikael frowned, setting the beer down so he could squat in front of Dean. A frown marred his handsome face, but it was one of worry and concern. Dean's stomach did another flip when Mikael rested a hand on his knee. He could feel the warmth of the man's skin, even through his jeans. How the hell the man was always so warm was beyond him. It was something he noticed anytime they happened to stand close to each other. No matter how cold it was, Mikael was always warm. He positively radiated warmth—literally.

"Hey." Mikael's voice was soft. "You were going through a lot when you got that envelope. Nobody is gonna blame you for not wanting to open it right then. And the instructions even told you not to open it yet. You were going through a significant loss at that point, and opening it would have meant letting go of that last little piece, right?"

Dean looked at the man, momentarily stunned by his insight. "Y-yeah, that's about right. But then I just forgot about it—forgot about all of it, including this place."

"Yeah, but you're here now, man. Hell, you've thrown everything you had into this place. You quit your job and packed up everything you had in your life, even your dog and that skittish-ass cat of yours. You threw it all in a truck and brought yourself out here. Every penny you saved up for who knows how long is going into this place. And you're personally working hard to bring it back with your own sweat and blood right now. Everything you've got is going into loving this farm, into making it what you want it to be. I never got to really meet or get to know your grandfather, but I know damn well that he'd be mighty proud of what you've done with the place."

Dean could only stare at Mikael for what seemed like ages. Mikael's hazel eyes gazed intently back at him, as if willing him to believe the words. It was hard to deny the man anything when he looked so damned earnest. Mikael's words warmed him, causing his stomach to flip again. How could a man who barely knew him speak of him so fondly? How could a man he barely knew suddenly seem like someone who knew him so well, someone to be trusted so easily?

"Thank you, Mikael," he said softly, smiling a little. He was thankful that the rush of emotions seemed to stay curled in his chest, rather than stinging the back of his eyes. As much as he appreciated the words and trusted Mikael—perhaps more than he should have—he didn't want to get all watery-eyed in front of him. He figured he'd had enough emotional moments in the past few weeks.

"Hey, it's just the truth. You ask me, you should be strutting around here like you own the place. Wait. You do own the place. Ehh, you know what I mean."

"It's alright, big guy. I know what you mean."

Mikael winked at him, standing up and giving him a final pat on his leg. Dean let out a small laugh, reaching up to pat the man's hip in mock consolation. Mikael's hand flicked to his for a moment, making Dean self-consciously pull his hand back a little. He hadn't really thought about it at the time—it was a simple gesture of affection. Now, he wondered if Mikael really did know about him and was weirded out by the sudden physical display.

Mikael made no comment, instead he glanced around with a thoughtful expression. Dean rarely saw that expression on Mikael's happy face. Sometimes, it was simply thoughtful, though there were moments—like now—where Mikael seemed a little sad. Whatever he was thinking, it was evidently taking him back to some point in time that Dean knew nothing about. The man didn't mind talking about personal things in Dean's life, but seemed to avoid anything hard or depressing about himself. Dean realized, despite all their talks, he knew very little about Mikael.

Mikael grunted, smirking a little. "Well, if you love a person like you've loved this place, someone's gonna be real lucky... heh. Oi, what are we all serious about? We've got movies to watch, don't we? C'mon already!"

Dean yelped in surprise as Mikael easily yanked him to his feet. Dean was by no means frail, but his size was nothing compared to the other man. Mikael had him beat in both height and weight by a considerable margin. Oddly enough it wasn't usually all that noticeable. Mikael never seemed overly imposing. It wasn't until moments like this— being yanked to his feet like he was a small child—that Dean was aware of the difference.

"Geez," he complained as he was pulled into the house, "just throw me around already."

"Naw, that's for after dinner and a movie. Don't you know how this works?" Mikael laughed and shot a wicked grin over his shoulder in Dean's direction.

Dean could only laugh, even if the thought brought about yet another little flutter to his stomach. The comment was probably just another playful joke coming from his new friend, but he couldn't help reacting, just a bit. He tampered down his emotions easily enough, and simply soaked up his friend's happy mood as he followed him into the house.

He managed to break himself free from Mikael's grip to pad into the kitchen. The sounds of Mikael greeting Jax in the living room filtered through as he preheated the oven. It wasn't particularly difficult for Jax to like someone. If they were willing to rub his belly and tell him he was a good boy, he was more than happy to be friends. A crash caught his attention as he shoved the pizza onto the rack.

"Hope that wasn't something expensive," he called through the house, raising a brow as he waited for a reply.

The sheepish reply came a moment later: "Oh no! Just... just a chair. We're good!"

Dean rolled his eyes, closing the oven door and setting the timer so he could check on it a little early. He didn't know if it was just because the oven was new or not, but the last one he'd made cooked to a crisp and fast. If he wasn't careful, all they'd have to eat tonight were whatever left-overs may still be edible in his fridge.

By the time he got back to the living room, everything looked suspiciously intact. Even Jax and Mikael were seated nicely on the couch, glancing innocently at Dean as he entered the room. Dean looked around to see what piece of furniture they'd damaged in their overly exuberant reunion. Finding nothing amiss, he sat down on the couch with a sigh, still glaring at the duo. Neither of them gave anything away—he saw only a warm smile from Mikael and a friendly butt wiggle from Jax.

"You two look far too innocent," Dean said.

"Perish the thought, my friend—oh look, the movie's starting!"

"Uh huh. Wouldn't have anything to do with the fact that you pushed the play button, would it?"

"Nope!" The cheery reply was followed by a shush as the movie began. Dean settled into the couch and let whatever little crime they had committed pass without further comment. If they'd truly broken something, he would eventually find it, probably when it was far too late to do anything about it.

They settled in well enough for the first movie, pausing it only so Dean could retrieve the pizza. After placing it carefully on the table in front of the couch and handing Mikael a beer, he settled back in. The movie resumed, and they contently sat there and watched it, chewing happily on the pizza and nursing their beers.

"I know I said it before, but you have a really badass setup," Mikael said, motioning to the TV and sound system and nodding in approval at the crystal-clear action on the screen.

Dean shrugged. "Told ya I didn't really do much socially, so I had plenty of money to spoil myself with nice toys like this. Turned out to be a good investment for me."

"It's kinda like your own personal mini movie theater. I always thought the whole Blu-Ray thing was just a scam to make ya pay thirty bucks for a movie you could get for half that in DVD. Guess I just need to get the right TV for it."

"You're just gonna watch porn on it if you do."

Mikael wrinkled his nose. "Nah, I hate porn."

Dean blinked. "Seriously? Thought you said you were a visual person?"

"Did I?" Mikael frowned, thinking back to when that might have come up. "Huh. Oh yeah, guess I did. But yeah, not the same thing at all. There is a big difference between people being paid to moan and grind on a screen for you and someone in front of you in real life grinding and moaning."

Suddenly, Dean was acutely aware of just how warm

Mikael was beside him, close enough to reach over and touch.

"Lord, I love that movie," Mikael exclaimed suddenly. The movie had ended. "I got another one and then we can watch one of your trash movies."

Dean snorted, heaving himself up to get another couple of beers while Mikael switched the movies out. By the time he returned, Mikael already had the movie menu up, ready to start the thriller he was apparently so damn fond of. Dean passed over a beer, smiling at Mikael's eagerness.

He'd given Mikael a hard time for being so excited over the movie, but in truth, he actually did like a lot of thriller movies—the ones that fell into the psychological thriller category, anyway, were second on his list of favorite genres. Mikael's favorite psychological legal drama had engrossed Dean quickly and burned away the next couple of hours.

"What'd ya think?" Mikael asked, glancing at Dean with a hopeful expression.

Dean nodded in approval. "That was really good, I have to admit. The dude plays a creep really well. Sure didn't expect it to go that way though, and I sure never thought I'd find myself cheering for a lawyer!"

Mikael gave a laugh. "Guess the moral of the story is don't pull the plug after you kill off your cheating wife, huh?"

Dean snorted. "I think it'd be best to just not shoot your wife at all. Divorce might be messier, but at least there's less chance of jail time."

"Dunno man, women," Mikael raised his brow, wiggling it a little.

"Lord, you get the beer. I'll choose the next movie."

Dean grinned at the man's heavy groan as he picked

himself up from the couch and made his way into the kitchen. The screen was already flashing to life as Mikael returned with an air of hesitancy. He huffed at the screen, where the main actress wielded a katana against unlikely foes and unlikely odds. Handing Dean a beer, he plopped onto the couch next to him, a little closer than he'd been before.

"Well, at least you chose a ridiculously over-the-top movie that's actually good. The soundtrack for this movie is good enough on its own."

"I'm so glad His Majesty is pleased. I figured I would save the good stuff for another time." He took a pull from his beer, then noticed Mikael's eyes on him. He felt a little self-conscious, as if he were buck naked. He might as well have been naked, based on way his stomach was flipping.

"Maybe we should just make this a one-time thing then," Mikael added as an afterthought, breaking Dean's weird feeling.

Dean laughed. "Yeah, yeah. You'll be back. They always come back."

Mikael's reply was lost as Dean started the movie and leaned back into the couch. He didn't know if they would really be able to make it to the second movie. Both were relatively lengthy, and it was already getting late for them. They hadn't been drinking too heavily, but both men were enjoying a nice light buzz from the beer. All in all, they were quite relaxed and enjoying themselves.

As the movie wore on, Dean and Mikael were all but sprawled across the couch. Their legs were pressed against one another, even though Jax was barely taking up any room on the far end of the couch. It was incredibly difficult for Dean to focus on the movie. He'd already seen the damn thing several times, so it wasn't like he was going to be missing anything. But at the same time, he wished the movie would distract him from Mikael's close presence.

This really wasn't what he needed. It took some willpower on his part, but he managed to subtly move his leg away from Mikael's, just enough so they weren't pressed against one another so tightly. It was a little foolish, and he felt like a teenager again, too bashful and hypersensitive for such a simple touch. Still, just that small gap between them was enough to calm him down, until Mikael shifted next to him again.

Mikael's leg pressed against Dean's once more. Dean could have groaned, if only out of frustration. He really didn't want to move again, in case Mikael noticed. The last thing he needed was for Mikael to think that he was intentionally moving away. The guy would either think that Dean was put off by physical contact—contact that Mikael probably saw as innocent affection—or he would realize exactly why Dean was so nervous with the touch, and he would become uneasy, too.

All Dean wanted out of the evening was to enjoy some nice quality time with his new friend. That was it. He didn't need this sudden rush of attraction to start making it difficult for him to be around the other man. He didn't think Mikael would go running for the hills if he suddenly realized that Dean was attracted to him. At least, Dean didn't want to think that, but he'd long since learned that people didn't always live up to one's expectations or hopes.

Suddenly, he had the feeling he was being watched. It was almost like when he was walking home last weekend. The sensation was sudden, piercing through his thoughts instantly. It was startling and a little out of place, considering he was comfortably—mostly comfortably—sitting in his own living room. When he finally glanced around for the source, he found Mikael staring at him. The shadows of the room gave Mikael that harsh look that Dean remembered seeing a few other times. It was powerful, and the flickering light from the movie wasn't helping much.

"Uh, Mikael?" he asked cautiously, both unnerved and inexplicably aroused by the man's concentrated expression.

Heat and pressure gripped his thigh, as Mikael's hand grasped his leg just above the knee. Dean jolted a little in surprise. He didn't move beyond the small jump, and Mikael's hand seemed to take that as encouragement. Work-strong fingers slid up his leg slowly. Dean's breathing was quickly becoming rough, his jeans tighter than they were only moments before.

"Mikael?" His voice was almost as fluttery as his stomach, and he swallowed hard.

"Guess it wasn't just me," Mikael finally said, catching Dean's eyes and pinning him to the spot. Before Mikael moved, Dean knew exactly what was going to happen. He was helpless in that split second, knowing that there was no way he was going to stop it. Even the simple touch of the man's hand on his leg had him short of breath. His gaze flicked to the man's lips, then to his eyes. A shiver ran through him as he drank in the intense gaze boring right into him.

Then Mikael did move. Twisting his body toward Dean, he pulled Dean in. Dean's surprised gasp at the rough treatment was cut off by the press of Mikael's mouth against his. The cry immediately turned into a moan that seemed to come from the deepest part of him. For a moment, the cautious part of his mind screamed that this was trouble and he should end it before it went too far. Then Mikael had one hand on his hip, holding tight, and the other cupping the back of his head. Any thoughts of stopping disappeared, and he finally responded to the touch, pressing himself up against Mikael.

The kiss was intense, more powerful than he had experienced in... well, he couldn't think clearly enough to remember. All he could do was open his mouth to let Mikael's tongue in. The casual, almost hesitant swipe of the man's tongue became bolder. Dean could sense Mikael feeling him out, testing his responses and driving for what worked. He could taste the beer as Mikael's tongue first explored his mouth and then began to claim it.

His hands roamed Mikael's body freely, greedily, responding heartily to his touch. Dean's hips rolled against that grip, pressing them up against the other man with a low groan that rumbled between the two of them. The sound was met with a growl from Mikael as he pushed against Dean's fighting hips, shoving them back down onto the couch. Dean gasped at the force, using his own hands to pull Mikael down on top of him.

The two of them continued, rutting against one another to the point that the constriction of Dean's jeans felt like they were squeezing the life out of his cock. The press of Mikael's groin against his own seemed to relieve the pressure, only to have it return before the next grinding thrust.

"Mikael," he gasped, hands fighting to get between them. Certainly Mikael had to be uncomfortable, as well. For a moment it seemed like Mikael might fight him, but instead, he relaxed enough to let Dean's hand slip between them. There wasn't much room to move his hand about yet he managed to find the man's cock and cup it. His brow shot up as his fingers slid along the denim-clad length, hardly able to articulate what he had found.

"Christ," was all he finally managed to get out, as he had to hunch to reach the tip. Mikael was definitely not lacking.

Nerves and excitement coiled through him as he explored it one more time with his fingertips. Mikael was apparently not the patient type, propping himself up enough to shove his hand between them and bat Dean's hand away. Dean sucked in a breath when he felt his pants being undone, then Mikael's, as the man fought with the fabric that separated them.

Suddenly, they were free, with a faint exhalation from each of them as the pressure eased. Just as Dean pushed his hips upward, Mikael's hand wrapped around him. Another moan and he pressed into the grip. He really wished he could see better in the dim light. He could feel Mikael's cock against him and could only reach down to grab-hold of it. His eager fingers curled around the thickness of the man's arousal, attempting to cover the full length of it as he stroked.

"Supplies?" Mikael asked, his voice low and rough, sending a chill down Dean's spine. Dean could only shake his head—all he had was lube upstairs. Not only did he not want either of them to leave this spot, he also didn't want to put them in a position where they had to consider potentially being unsafe. As much as he wanted to throw caution to the wind and hop atop Mikael, it was not the best idea—kind of like what they were already doing.

"It's fine," Mikael grunted. "We ain't lasting long like this anyway." He didn't sound unhappy. In fact, he bent forward as he stroked Dean, his teeth sinking into the muscles of Dean's shoulder. Dean cried out, feeling the faint pain twist with the pleasure of the man's hand on his cock, his thumb gliding across the slick head.

Mikael pushed back, shoving at both of their pants. The struggle only lasted a few moments before their jeans were off. Dean was both amused and not at all surprised to see that the other man didn't necessarily believe in underwear, his whole lower body was now bare. There was that thrill of pleasure again at the sight of the man's cock, illuminated by the TV. Christ, he was both happy and a little disappointed that Mikael barely paid attention to Dean's boxers, pushing himself between Dean's legs, eager to proceed. Their cocks slid together as Mikael moved himself forward, rutting against him once more. Dean continued to moan, as Mikeal came down on him pushing their bodies against one another yet again. His mouth opened as Mikael pressed his own against him hungrily.

Dean didn't know what he was more aware of—the feel of their cocks against one another, or the man's hard body pressing and shifting against his. Dean might have had nothing to be ashamed about when it came to his body, but Mikael seemed sculpted out of rock. Scrabbling up the man's back, his fingers found the lines of Mikael's muscles. His fingers rolled and dipped, as his hands roamed up and down the man's back before firmly holding onto his hips.

The larger man's grip fell around their cocks once more as he continued to thrust against Dean. He was already almost to his limit as it was. The man felt way too good at that moment, and his taste was still in his mouth. Mikael's mouth had already moved on, nipping at any part of Dean that he could find. His other hand was propped across Dean's chest to both hold him in place and keep himself steady.

"M-Mikael," Dean gasped, hardly able to speak as the man thrust again, timing it with another sharp nip at his throat.

"Cum," the other man growled.

The command went straight to Dean's core. His body responded to it quicker than his mind did, which was saying something. It only took a few more pumps before his body finally began to coil and tighten. Gasping out Mikael's name one more time, he thrust his hips hard up into the man's grip. Warmth spread across his torso as he came in spurts, fingers digging into the muscles of the man's neck.

His head swam and he began to sink back into the couch, the relaxing effect of the orgasm already beginning to hit him. Then his cock was released and Mikael's mouth was on him. Against Mikael's body, Dean could feel the smoother glide as the man stroked himself. Dean's cock, barely past its orgasm, gave an interested twitch when he realized Mikael was using his cum as lube. He responded to the kiss with a great deal more vigor than he thought he had left in his body.

A growl came from Mikael, his teeth catching Dean's bottom lip as his hips jerked. Warmth hit his chest. Mikael's orgasm shuddered through him as he painted the two of them with his cum. His body rippled above Dean, who couldn't restrain the moan wrung out of him. The warmth of their cum mingling was both soothing and erotic. Then the tension fled from Mikael's body, and he sagged.

Dean was amazed when Mikael found the strength to push himself up off the couch. He was confused, and maybe a little hurt, that the man got up so quickly. Then he saw him coming back with the towel he'd tossed over his leather recliner earlier in the day. Chuckling, Dean accepted the towel and cleaned himself up before handing it back for Mikael to do the same, ogling the man as he cleaned himself up in the flickering light of the TV.

Dean gestured lazily when Mikael held up the towel. Mikael shrugged and tossed it to the floor before crawling back onto the couch. Dean grunted in halfhearted protest as he was shifted about. Apparently, the other man wasn't above giving a cuddle or two after he got them both off. Mikael pushed between Dean and the back of the couch, arms wrapping him up and holding him tightly.

Mikael grunted into Dean's ear, nuzzling his neck. Dean couldn't suppress the smile he felt spreading across his lips as Mikael's body relaxed against his, breaths evening out. He'd never had the chance to see Mikael asleep before but, somehow wasn't surprised that he was the type to fall asleep quickly. Even though he wasn't a morning person, Dean normally wasn't quite that easy to knock out—his brain liked to keep him up throughout the night, when it could. Work on the farm had done wonders for exhausting his mind.

The orgasm was helping with that too. He probably could have still fought sleep, but the warmth of the man at his back and the comforting press of the arms around his chest was too much. The steady rhythm of Mikael's breathing was all he could really hear after a little while. It was unbelievably soothing to a man who normally loathed sharing his sleeping space with more than his pets. His eyelids grew heavy, his own breathing syncing up to Mikael's as he slowly drifted off into a comfortable, easy sleep.

6

*W*hen Dean had woken the next morning, sprawled awkwardly on the couch, he was alone. Vague remnants of strange dreams in his head, involving running and the moon, were all that lingered. Dean wasn't sure how Mikael had managed to get disentangled and off the couch without waking him up, not to mention the fact that the man's truck was loud enough to wake the dead.

But when Dean padded into the kitchen to start up his coffee, it was nearly done brewing. Not quite fully awake, he had blinked at the device, trying to figure it out. Either Mikael had left quite recently, or the man had made a great guess at what time Dean would be waking up. Either way, he had left a note beside the coffee maker, promising to see Dean again come Monday morning. It had ended with a smiley face to accent the point. Dean wasn't quite sure what to make of it, but he wasn't going to figure it out with a sleep-fogged mind.

He would have preferred to have spent the rest of the day pretending that what happened hadn't fazed him, but that would have been a stone-cold lie. Sure, half the time he was okay, going about his business in the house. His weekend time was reserved to both relax and to continue opening boxes and decorating the house.

Yet he spent half of that time fretting over what had happened. Sure, it hadn't gone as far as it could have. But he wasn't going to stand around and pretend that the memory of the man's lips against his didn't have his body humming with a strange energy all over again. The fact that Mikael hadn't hung around afterward left him nervous. The note by the coffee maker helped to temper that, but there was still a part of him that worried over the implications of the man just up and leaving like he had, without a word of explanation.

All in all, he was feeling both high on life and stressed beyond belief. He couldn't remember the last time he'd felt something like this, something so contradictory that it drove him half insane. There was no point anymore in pretending he wasn't interested in the man. Their physical chemistry had been off the charts. Mikael was many things, but the sheer fact that Dean already had a great deal of trust in him, that the man could make him laugh so easily, talk so freely, and just feel completely at home in his company, spoke volumes about how Dean felt.

Chiding himself for behaving like some love-struck teenager who didn't know how to deal with infatuation, he tried to throw himself into his work. It didn't really help much, but it did do wonders for passing the time. The motivation to distract himself certainly provided ample energy for unpacking and setting things up. By the time he climbed into bed that night, he was sure he had accomplished more with the house in that one day than he had managed in the entire time he'd been back.

His dreams were no less strange that night, either. When the alarm woke him on Monday morning, he couldn't clearly remember them, but he felt disconcerted. The presence of Jax's body next to him gave him a start, the feel of his fur confusing him for a moment. The mutt cocked his head wearily at his master, perhaps wondering as Dean was, what exactly was wrong. Chuckling at himself, he flipped the alarm off and scratched Jax's ears as an apology. He certainly envied the dog's ability to simply roll over and go back to sleep; Dean could afford no such luxury.

By the time Mikael had rolled up the path to the house and hopped from his truck, Dean was already in his customary spot on the front porch. The mornings were getting warmer with each passing day, and he no longer needed a blanket or jacket on top of the coffee he drank. He was also so full of nervous energy that he didn't think he really needed something extra to keep him warm. Come to think of it, he probably didn't need the coffee giving him extra jitters, either.

"Morning!" Mikael called, hopping to the ground and grabbing his chest of tools as usual before strolling up to the porch. Dean was immediately aware that the other man, while appearing his usual chipper self, seemed a bit off. If Dean didn't know any better, he would swear the other man was watching him cautiously.

"Good morning, Flight Risk," Dean replied with a small smile.

Mikael's brow shot up into his hairline. "Flight Risk? Damn, right to the point, aren't you?"

Dean wanted to wince, but shrugged instead. "First thing that entered my head. You know I'm not really too thoughtful when I'm groggy."

"But you look more awake than I've ever seen you at this hour."

"Maybe I'm finally just getting used to this morning routine thing."

"Oh? After only what... ten years of it? Take your time don't ya?"

Dean said nothing, though he did smile a little. He might not have approached the problem as smoothly as he would have wished, but he had done it. If it was going to be totally addressed, he would wait until Mikael was willing to meet him in the middle on it. It certainly hadn't done anything to dissipate the nervous energy boiling away in his chest.

After a moment's pause, Mikael sighed, "Alright, I took off."

"You did."

"It wasn't for the reason you think, though."

"No?"

Mikael frowned at Dean's raised brow. "Okay, well, not totally for that reason."

"Uh huh." Dean smiled a little. "How about you just tell me what's going on in that crazy head of yours. We can go from there."

That brought a grin to the face of the larger man. "That's fair. Alright, so yeah, I took off because of what we did. I mean, I kinda wondered about you from like... well pretty much the first time we met. Not that you like, gave yourself away... just, you know... something told me. I dunno. Anyways, I didn't think even if you were, that it would be a thing. I mean, you're a hot man, but I wasn't gonna go jumping ahead of myself or anything. But then Saturday night happened and... well... I bailed. I don't get to do that sort of thing much, you know? And it's never been in town. I've always had to go out of my way for that."

Dean squinted, trying to keep up with the sudden expulsion of information and explanation. "So, what you're saying is, you bailed because you were wigged out that I actually screwed around with you, and because I'm from town?"

Mikael looked a little bashful. "Sort of. I mean, I've been with other people before, but it was... different with you. More fun."

Dean had to smile at that, catching the man's gaze, even if it did cause his stomach to flip. "Agreed."

Mikael blinked. "Really?"

"What?" Dean asked, laughing a little. "Did you think you were the only one?"

"I mean, I hoped you had fun and shit, but I figured I had freaked you out or something."

"How... how does someone who pinned me to the couch, ordered me about, and took total control suddenly turn bashful?"

Mikael rubbed the back of his head. "Magic?"

"Look," Dean said, unable to hold the laugh, "I almost wondered if I'd snagged me a straight guy who just got curious and went through with it one time. The first time I saw you I thought you were straight—hot, but straight. Then you go and do all that with me the other night and it was... ah... yeah, it was fun, but then you were gone."

"You thought I was hot?" Mikael asked, looking over at Dean curiously.

That made Dean smile again. "Yeah, I did. And I pretty much wanted to jump you from the moment I saw you. Then we became friends, or whatever, and that... didn't help too much, actually."

"Friends or whatever?" This time, it was Mikael's turn to smirk.

"Yeah, or whatever." Dean's voice was strained and he felt the heat rush to his face. He realized he had voiced his own concerns over the nature of their relationship. For all he'd known, Mikael considered Dean as cool and someone he didn't mind being around occasionally, not exactly a friend. Dean hadn't wanted to impose his own feelings on the other man by making claims of friendship.

"I'd say we're friends, yeah," Mikael assured him, his expression warm as he regarded Dean.

"Friends who had fun."

"Friends who definitely had some fun."

"Friends who had fun and could have some more... or just friends?" Dean asked, now knowing it was time to approach that particular avenue. If Mikael didn't want to continue with what they had started Saturday night, Dean wasn't going to insist on it. If he had to choose between sex with the man or the man's friendship, he would choose the latter without hesitation. The physical chemistry between them had been amazing, but the rest of the chemistry was way better.

Mikael raised a brow. "You wanna do more?"

Dean really did blush at the question this time. "Yeah... of course. But only if you're game."

Mikael laughed. "When a guy like you says that they wanna be both my friend and sleep with me, I'm not gonna say no."

"I'm thinking you have that a little backwards. There's no way I'd be able to tell you no."

"Oh?" Dean could see a familiar emotion behind those hazel eyes. He had only seen it one time, but he already recognized it from the other night. He had thought it was just a trick of the low light, but out here in the sun, the look was predatory. It really should have been unnerving to see that, especially to see it on the face of a man who was normally so warm and jovial. Instead, it pooled heat in his gut, and he could already feel the blood rushing to his groin.

"What?" Dean asked, playing dumb, though he did feel struck dumb, in a way.

Mikael set the toolbox down on the step. Dean watched with wide eyes as Mikael came closer and knelt before him, pushing his legs apart so that he was between them. Mikael's eyes fell on the bulge in Dean's pants. His strong fingers pushed his legs further apart and with more dexterity than Dean felt he would have been able to manage —his pants were undone and pushed away from his hips in seconds.

"Mikael," he tried, not quite sure at that moment what he really wanted to say.

Mikael ignored him, save for a smirk shot in his direction. Dean forgot whatever he was going to say as the man's hand slipped into his underwear, gripping his shaft, and pulling him free. He barely had a moment to register the touch before Mikael's mouth was around him once more. Where the other night had been done in shadows with the faint light from the TV, the morning light left no detail unclear.

Mikael's mouth slid over the head of his cock and down his shaft effortlessly. For a man who claimed to have only gotten some fun occasionally, he had apparently learned enough. Dean groaned, flopping back against the back of the chair as he witnessed Mikael's mouth slide completely over his arousal. He groaned as the man came back up and looked right into Dean's eyes.

"Jesus," Dean groaned. "Don't do that. I'm not gonna last long."

Which, in terms of wanting to last, was the worst thing he could have said, apparently. Mikael drove down with more vigor than before, sucking Dean to the back of his throat and letting the muscles work over the sensitive head before pulling back once more. Dean writhed in the chair, unable to stop his hips from pushing up into Mikael's face.

Encouraging the movement, Mikael picked up the pace while making sure to keep Dean's cock deep in his throat as often as possible. His fingers slipped under Dean's ass, gripping hard and pushing his hips up. Dean was the one who had the hard time maintaining eye contact, hardly able to keep his eyes open as he tried to focus on lasting. Mikael was having none of it, however, working his hardest to drag Dean over the edge.

Dean knew it was a losing battle. His body was betraying him quickly. He sputtered, feeling his muscles coiling up, his breathing becoming more difficult. Repeating the man's name, he tried to warn Mikael, whose only response was to increase his speed, working the muscles of his throat even more passionately. It was too much for Dean, who, with a final cry, shoved his hips upward into Mikael's mouth. It felt like the cum poured out of him as he hung there, suspended in the moment of his orgasm.

When it was over, he slumped back in the chair with a faint groan. Mikael chuckled, sliding his lips gently away from Dean's now-softening cock. Dean was faintly aware that the man was kindly tucking him back into his pants, though he left the actual fastening to Dean. Then, there was the presence of the man's lips on his own once more. Dean gave a faint groan tasting himself on Mikael's tongue.

Responding to the kiss, he reached up to caress the man's collarbone.

"Mmm, better than coffee, eh?" Mikael chuckled again against Dean's lips.

"Christ," Dean swore, a little shaky. "If that's what I can expect, I'll give up the coffee completely."

"That... is probably the best compliment anyone has ever given me," Mikael said, frowning in what appeared to be confusion.

Dean only laughed, adjusting his pants and eyeing Mikael's own crotch. Much as he had enjoyed the man's impromptu blowjob, he was also thinking he might like to have some fun of his own. Dean was certainly not the type to pick his partner based on size, but you had to appreciate the good ones when you saw them. Mikael was undeniably impressive, and Dean was eager to have his hands and mouth on it once more.

"Take care of it at lunch," Mikael hummed, nipping at Dean's jaw line playfully. "We've still got work to do."

Dean huffed at the other man, making a last-ditch effort to grab at him and prevent him from getting away. He wanted to get his hands, and mouth, on what Mikael had to offer. The other man laughed and danced out of reach, cocking a brow expectantly at Dean, who could only sigh in resignation before heaving himself up out of the chair with a deep breath. Mikael was right—they did have work to do.

Work was easier said than done. Even if his work didn't necessarily keep him near the other man, he found that his eyes were remarkably good at locating Mikael, no matter where he was on the property. It was certainly distracting, and he had a difficult time keeping his mind on the farm. Rather, he thought of the shape of the man's body in the sunlight, or the way his muscles moved and bunched as he hefted the wood about. He was also pretty sure that Mikael knew he was being watched and was doing everything in his power to pretend to ignore it.

By the time Mikael shouted across the property that he was hungry, and that Dean better hurry his city ass up for some grub, Dean was more than ready. He suspected that Mikael would purposefully make him wait until after they had eaten. The guy certainly seemed to get off on teasing him.

But when they were in his kitchen, getting ready to make their sandwiches, Mikael gave in instantly when Dean's hands grabbed a hold of him and pushed him against the counter. Mikael had apparently been anticipating the moment, if the shape his cock made in his jeans was any indication. Dean wasted no time on foreplay or niceties either. Opening the man's pants and fishing Mikael's cock out, he went right to work. There was no way he would be able to take the man completely in his throat, but he'd be damned if he wouldn't give it a half ass try.

Mikael had no complaints, his grip on the counter never wavering, only tightening. Dean felt considerably better about how quickly he had shot off that morning when Mikael finally lost it. The other man hadn't lasted much longer than Dean had, cum pumping into Dean's mouth and throat in a matter of minutes. Dean had moaned hungrily around the man's cock, taking a few more slides into his mouth until Mikael pushed him away with a laugh at the sensitivity.

Dean looked up from his place on the floor in front of Mikael and smirked. "Okay, we can have food now."

Mikael chuckled, running his fingers through Dean's short hair as Dean picked himself up from the ground. The man's strong fingers curled around his head and slid down, playing along his neck as he stood. Mikael was quite tactile it seemed, and Dean wasn't going to argue. It made him feel like Mikael couldn't quite get enough of touching him, and he rather liked it that way.

Mikael's eyes widened, his mouth twisting for the barest of moments as he jerked his hand back away from Dean. The motion took Dean by surprise, and if it wasn't for the fact that the man's eyes were still on him, he would have been worried that someone or something was behind him.

"Mikael?" he asked, reaching to brush the spot where Mikael had just touched him. He found only warm flesh and then the coolness of metal as his fingers brushed along the silver chain of his grandfather's necklace. He grasped it out of reflex, letting his fingers slide down to the pendant and held it tight in his grip.

"I'm okay," Mikael said with a laugh, waving him off. "Just get a twinge in my back sometimes. Ain't nothing to worry about."

"Looked like more than a twinge." Dean's eyes widened when he spotted a flash of angry red skin on the man's hand. "Hey, when did you hurt your hand?"

Mikael looked down at the hand as if in surprise, curling it into a fist as he shrugged. "Burned it this morning making breakfast. It ain't a big deal, don't worry about it. Nice necklace."

Dean fidgeted with the pendant a moment before giving a shrug. "Yeah, it was my grandfather's."

Mikael nodded. "Silver?"

"Yeah, I can't wear gold. Maybe white gold, but not the regular kind."

"How come?"

"I have an allergic reaction to it. Been that way since I was a kid, actually. I used to know what the symbol on this necklace is, but I haven't been able to think of it quite yet. Just nice to wear it though, to have a piece of him with me now and again."

"Fenrir," Mikael replied almost instantly.

"Fenrir?" Dean asked. He pulled the pendant up for a closer look. "That Norse monster wolf, you mean?"

Mikael laughed a little. "He was a god, actually, who also happened to be a big-ass wolf. He was supposed to tear things up when the apocalypse came, and of course, he was supposed to be slain after that, too. So..."

"Ragnarok," Dean said thoughtfully, remembering his mythology enough to pull that word from the depths of his mind. "So, Grandpa had a necklace of some old Viking wolf god..."

Mikael shrugged, opening his hand in a helpless gesture. "Maybe your grandfather was more old school than you thought?"

Dean eyed him for a moment, looking quickly back at the injured hand. Mikael spotted his gaze and flipped his hand around to hide the red line. As laid back and patient as Mikael could be, Dean had already spotted the stubborn streak that was a mile wide.

"You gonna just keep telling me to not worry about your various body problems then?" Dean asked.

"Yep!" Mikael exclaimed with a grin. He motioned to the counter. "Weren't you making us lunch?"

Dean narrowed his eyes, poking the man in the chest. "Look mister, if you think I'm going to start waiting on you hand and foot just bec—"

Mikael leaned forward and kissed him sweetly on his lips. Dean's breath shook as Mikael's hazel eyes met his dark ones. Mikael smiled softly. "Please?"

There was nothing to do but sigh. "That's cheating, but effective."

He heard Mikael hum happily as he turned with a hidden smile to start making up their lunch. The sounds of the man making his way down the hallway while talking to Jax followed, making him smile even more than before. Dean knew that this was a casual thing, and that they were going to remain only friends. Even if those friends did occasionally have a bit of naked fun together.

Yet he already knew that he was lost, regardless if it was a good idea. No, he wasn't in love, but he was certainly hooked on the other man. Maybe it was just the loneliness of years spent virtually on his own, combined with finally having a connection with someone. Maybe it was just Mikael. Dean didn't know. What he did know was that the man's laugh was infectious and that his smile warmed him. Hell, they hadn't done much more than fool around a little and yet it was amazing—everything, from the feel of the man's skin, to the deep, earthy smell that always seemed to hang around him. Dean had always thought that using smell to describe someone you were intimate with was strange, but not now.

Not even a day into their new arrangement, he was already breaking the rules. That was fine, though. He would deal with it as it happened, and he would try to keep it from interfering in their fun or their friendship. The last thing he wanted was to scare Mikael off with all that nonsense of attachments and intimacy. There was no need to add complications just because he was getting a small crush on the man, even if that crush seemed to be getting bigger by the hour.

Right?

Right.

7

"That's an interesting picture." Mikael's voice caught Dean's attention, pulling him away from his drifting thoughts. They were sprawled on opposite ends of the couch. Dean had been in the process of trying to get his brain to start functioning properly again. Mikael had worked him over quite well with their last bit of fun, and Dean was finding it hard to regain his senses. He had spent the past several minutes of silence trying to achieve just that.

"Hmm?" he hummed in question, finally picking his head up enough to eye the other man. It had only been a week since their new arrangement began, but Mikael seemed to be quite at ease. He certainly looked both comfortable and highly appealing, leaning back and relaxed on the arm of the couch. Once Dean was able to think a little more clearly, he would do his best to try to appreciate what he was seeing.

Damn, the man looked good naked.

"The painting," Mikael explained patiently, with a little smile, pointing over behind them. Dean had to pick himself up to see what Mikael was gesturing at. His body protested the movement, clearly wanting to continue relaxing. When Dean spied the painting, he laughed and laid back into the comforting folds of the couch.

"I think it's a companion piece to a couple of the others that are around here," he explained. "My grandfather kept them throughout the house. I decided to put that one there."

Like the others, the painting used dark tones with a few bright colors thrown in. A lone man stood, his back to a blazing fire, facing outward before a large patch of darkening woods as twilight took over the sky. From the tree line, there came the faint yet identifiable shapes of wolves prowling from the haven of the trees. The man stood, a large walking stick in hand, his other hand extended outward toward the pack in an obvious gesture of calming welcome.

"There are others?" Mikael asked.

"Yeah, there's one where, I'm pretty sure it's the same guy, walking with what I think is the same pack of wolves. Another is just a bunch of men dancing and singing around a fire."

"Sounds like a story."

"It is. My grandfather told it to me a few times at night when I was a kid."

Mikael smiled. "Tell it to me."

Dean shifted. "Uh, it's been a little while, so I might not remember it too well."

"That's alright. Just tell me."

All he could do was sigh and think back to the last time his grandfather had told him that story. Fittingly enough, they had been outside, near the woods, staring into a fire much like the one in the painting. It had been his last summer at the farm and he was going into his senior year of

high school. After that, he'd been caught up in putting his
life together, setting it up for the future. He was so sure of
his future then, with no idea of the tragedy that was going to
come his way.

"Our family has been on this land for quite a while," he
began, "well before anyone from Europe ever thought of
coming over here to live."

"Explains the skin," Mikael joked, brushing his fingers
along Dean's newly tanned skin.

Dean laughed a little, catching the man's finger playfully.
"A little bit, but I'm kind of separated from it by a few generations. Grandfather never told me what the name of the
tribe was that we came from, though. He always said that
names have more power than we think. But they apparently
weren't a tribe you'd find in any books."

Mikael's eyes found his. "A mystery. Alright, so what was
so important about this tribe?"

"Honestly? My grandfather was pretty vague about
things like that when I was younger. Said he'd tell me in due
time, if he thought I was ready to know. He knew a great
deal about a lot, but he also had some strange beliefs, too.
Even my mom didn't know what to think of it. Truth be told,
it wasn't until after I was in college that I even learned he'd
never told her half the stuff he'd told me. Over the phone,
he just said that he never got the right 'feeling' from her.
Whatever that meant."

"Feeling?"

"Yeah, he wouldn't explain." Dean traced over the
memories and stories flitting through his mind.

"Okay," Mikael said slowly, propping himself up a little
higher. "So what did he tell you about the tribe?"

Dean managed to rouse himself from his old memories
and continued. "They had been here for quite a while.

There were stories in the tribe about watching... Well, Grandpa called it Luna. But, watching Luna come to be in the sky above them."

Mikael's brow rose. "They claimed to know when the moon showed up?"

"Well, not when exactly. There wasn't really a timetable on the stories. But yeah, there was a story about the fire that lit the skies, the dark clouds in the sky. Ya know, pretty much everything you would expect from something huge hitting the planet. Don't know if I really believe it, and can't say I know that much about science to say if that's remotely accurate or even possible."

Mikael said nothing, only watching Dean as he continued.

"Anyway, Grandpa said that Luna coming to life in the sky heralded a new age for their people. Now, you could see at night sometimes, but it apparently also brought... power."

"Power?"

Dean grinned. "Moon magic. Well, not really, but apparently the moon showing up awakened something in the tribe. Grandpa wasn't too clear, but it caused some differences in the tribe, and they split apart after that. Dunno what happened to the ones who left, but the ones that stayed were better at living off the land. Every one of them was 'wise in the ways of the land.' Basically, they were really good at maintaining the land, growing stuff, taking care of animals. Stuff like that."

Mikael eyed Dean carefully, a hint of a smile on his otherwise serious face. "So, your ancestors said that the moon made them really good farmers?"

Dean laughed. "Yeah, pretty much. I mean there were stories of individuals who could do more than just grow things really well. They could actually 'speak' to the land,

and even some of the animals. I don't know the full range of powers they claimed to have, but these few were really tuned into the earth and the land. They were highly respected by their people, kinda like how a shaman or medicine man would be in some other part of the world. Except they didn't talk to spirits, they dealt with the physical, the land."

Mikael looked thoughtful. "So, the moon made them really good farmers and sometimes badass Druids?"

"I think you've been watching fantasy movies too much. I didn't think the Druids in Europe were like that, but what do I know? It wasn't like random magical beliefs were something I really studied. I took a different elective."

"What? Fucking 101?" Mikael asked with a devilish grin on his face.

"Actually, yeah," Dean chuckled. "Human Sexuality was offered, so I took it. It was interesting enough and not too difficult, so it was an easy credit."

"I'm guessing they didn't give hands-on lessons, either," Mikael said, eyeing the other man with a familiar look.

Dean held up a warning finger. "Don't you dare, horn dog. I'm still recovering. Let me get some of my energy back before you decide to attack."

"Fine," Mikael replied in a drawn-out way. "Was that all your grandfather told you?"

"No. There was more. Our people, after generations, discovered another tribe. These people had been changed by the coming of Luna, as well, but it was their spirits that had been changed. See, apparently something had happened with the coming of Luna had fused the spirit of beasts inside these men and women."

"Beasts?"

"Yeah. They could walk as men and women, or they

could walk as the beasts that they were imbued with. It didn't stop at just one generation, obviously, since they had been like that, or so they claimed, since the coming of Luna. They gained strength the stronger Luna was, so I'm thinking that meant full or not full moon. Our people were the opposite, the less strong that Luna was, the better everything our people had apparently picked up would be."

Mikael's frown deepened, "Why the opposite?"

"Ya know, I asked Grandpa about that once, and all he said was 'Sol.'"

"Soul?"

Dean laughed, "No, not 'soul', Sol. S-o-l. A name some people have used for the sun. Like I said, he didn't go into it much, but he said our people thrived on the strength of the sun and the weakness of the moon. This other tribe was the total opposite."

Mikael thought on that for a moment, nodding slowly. "Okay, so what happened?"

"People are people, I guess, no matter the generation. Who would have thought? Anyways, there was a lot of fighting that went down between the two tribes. Both wanted to claim the land as theirs, and nobody was willing to share. Eventually, some big ass thing happened that made them stop trying to kill each other. Grandpa called it a 'bond that crossed the boundaries of hate and distrust.' Don't ask me what. Probably some Romeo and Juliet stuff. Even the mystical people of history were suckers for a romance, but whatever it was, it did the trick. They made peace long enough to sit down, talk things over, and eventually came to an agreement."

"Wait, so these people had just fought one another for no reason, then made up for some other reason?" Mikael asked. His confusion evident.

Dean shook his head. "It wasn't for *no* reason. Both wanted the land—it was apparently very special. But I remember Grandpa saying something once about 'others.' I don't know who the 'others' were, but not all of the people who were changed by Luna turned out all that great. He told me that I should remember this... that 'magic isn't good or evil, it just is. But sometimes it can get twisted up, by accident or choice, and people are the same way.' I'm guessing there wasn't a lot of land like it, and they had a border dispute. They made up only because they were both losing people and didn't want to get wiped out."

"Well, aren't you the cynical one?" Mikael asked with another laugh.

"No, that's just how a lot of battles and wars in history go. Everyone has their reasons for the war, but then there's the story they tell afterward to make it all seem better. Just look at how two people are after they fight, then apply it to whole countries or nations." Dean shrugged. He didn't consider it cynical, just realistic.

"That's fair," Mikael agreed, his fingers now tracing a circle on Dean's calf. "So?"

Dean was finding himself a little distracted by the other man's touch. Even this light gesture was enough to make it difficult to focus on anything but the movements of the man's fingers on his skin. This was so much more than a normal rebound reaction to him having been deprived of real human contact like this for so long. It was all about this man, and he damn well knew it. He was already tumbling down a long path that would probably bring him nothing but trouble, and maybe more than a little heartache.

"So, what did they settle on?" Mikael persisted, poking Dean playfully.

"Oh! Well, because of their differences, they settled on

an arrangement. The people, who could talk to the earth, the Listeners, would use their gifts to care for the land and share its bounty. They would keep an eye out for dangers to the land when the other tribe wasn't up to full strength. The Listeners became the Watchers. But the others—Luna's Children—agreed to be the brawn of the operation. They could have contact with the spirit world because they were two spirits in one body, but they were... well, if you can turn into an animal with a human mind, it makes ya pretty scary. So, they became the Guardians, the ones who would defend the land from outsiders—and the 'others.'"

"Huh," Mikael grunted. "And that worked?"

"I guess it appeared to work pretty well for them, because that was the story that kept getting passed down, even long after everyone forgot what this place looked like before it was settled by the Europeans. Now, it's just a story that gets told now and again. There's probably some family member of mine out there somewhere who know these stories, but I wouldn't know who to even ask."

He noted the serious look on Mikael's face. The man truly appeared to be giving everything he had just said some serious thought. Even more, he looked as if he were analyzing Dean, trying to find something. Dean hadn't thought the old stories were anything more than amusing tales passed down through the generations. Even when he was a boy and his grandfather had first told the story of the coming of Luna, he hadn't taken them seriously. Stories were stories. They weren't the same thing as reality.

"Hey, you're looking way too serious over some old stories," Dean said, cocking his head at the other man curiously.

Mikael looked closely at him. "Don't you think there's some truth to them?"

Dean blinked. He hadn't expected Mikael would be so fascinated. "Well, yeah. I mean, there might be something to the part of them being around when the moon showed up. Like I said, I don't know my science well enough to know if people were even around back then. But everything else? C'mon, I don't believe any of that. It's just fun."

"I bet your grandfather was a believer."

"Well, yeah." Dean shifted uncomfortably. "But that's Grandpa for you. He wasn't a stupid man, and he was nobody's fool, that's for sure. But that doesn't mean he wasn't allowed to believe some strange things... and he did. And just because I respected him doesn't mean I'm going to go along with every strange belief he had. Maybe he wanted me to believe them a little, I don't know, but I don't."

Mikael nodded slowly. The thoughtful expression on the man's face was confusing Dean. Did he actually believe what Dean had just told him? There was no reason to believe any of it, really. Every family had their old stories, and there were plenty of strange and weird things passed down by different types of people, all over the world. If even a quarter of those legends and myths were true, the world would be overrun with monsters and all kinds of craziness. He didn't really know too much about different aspects of science, but he certainly knew it did a better job of explaining the world than anything else he'd heard in his time on Earth.

"Hey." Dean nudged Mikael again. "Are you... believing all that stuff?"

"Maybe." Mikael grinned suddenly, the grave expression on his face disappearing in an instant. His fingers found their way back to Dean's legs, sliding forward. Dean grunted in surprise, leaning forward to accept the kiss the other man laid on him. Fire lit in his gut again, and he leaned back as

Mikael pushed him down onto the couch. "But more importantly, I believe we're both up for Round Two."

Dean laughed, letting Mikael spread his legs, their conversation quickly forgotten as he watched Mikael dip low.

8

"So, you've never told me about your family," Dean said finally, breaking the silence between them. They sat on the porch, which was now repaired, watching the sun setting in the distance. In the few weeks that had passed since they had begun their little arrangement, the two of them spent a lot of their free time together. This also meant that they were often physically close. Dean rather liked that he could sit next to Mikael on the steps, leaning against him ever so lightly, taking advantage of the warmth of the other man's body as they relaxed.

Mikael shifted away slightly and gazed down at Dean with an inscrutable expression. "No, not really. It's not something I talk about too often, ya know?"

Dean nodded. They'd shared quite a bit back and forth, but this was one topic that Mikael had never broached. Dean had certainly picked up on the fact that there was more to the story than a simple shrug and an easy smile. He'd been around the man enough now to see when Mikael was sidestepping something that was truly bothering him.

Mikael sighed. "We... we just don't see eye-to-eye on

things."

"Things?" Dean asked, not wanting to say too much if Mikael might start talking.

"Yeah, mostly about what I'm doing with my life. If you think Town people are a little ridiculous about things, you should see people in The Grove. They're not all quite as strict as my family, but there are plenty who are. They don't think we should have too much to do with 'outsiders,' as they call them. It's stupid."

Dean cocked his head, then realized he had unconsciously adopted one of Mikael's gestures. "So, I'm guessing they weren't too big on you taking up a job in town?"

"That's a pretty mild way of putting it," Mikael snorted. "We're big on family and community, though. That's probably the only thing that keeps my parents from going too crazy on me. They still ain't happy about it, but at least they've stopped bringing it up every day."

Dean frowned, looking out at the work that Mikael had done in the past few weeks. The coops were up, the barn repaired, and an extra storage shed had even been put together. The house had been repaired, both inside and out, and the outside was painted and fresh. The fence was rebuilt. Hell, the man had even made a nice new mailbox for the end of the driveway leading from his property to the road. Between all of that and the work he'd done himself, plus the crops in the field and the animals milling about, the place finally looked complete.

"I would think they'd be a little proud, at least," he said finally, still frowning. "You helped me put this place back together. I couldn't have done this without you, you know."

Mikael smiled a little. "I'm glad you're happy with how it turned out. It means that you can really be settled in, and I know that's what you wanted from the start."

Dean nodded, entwining his fingers with Mikael's. The other man glanced down at their hands, staring at the sight in silence. Dean supposed that he probably should have been a little more cautious with his displays of affection. There hadn't been much of a change in the way that they did things. Hell, they hadn't even fucked yet, though Dean had privately bought the lube and condoms they would need. The only thing that had really changed had been his feelings. While Mikael seemed as relaxed and at home with their arrangement as ever, Dean's feelings had only deepened. It wasn't the best of situations to have gotten himself into, but who could ever control how they felt?

Perhaps it wasn't totally true that Mikael had stayed the same about everything. Dean had been growing increasingly worried as the man finished up his projects on the house. With each passing day, Mikael grew quieter as they drew closer to the time he no longer needed to be working on the farm. This was his last day of work. It was all finished. Mikael had been almost completely silent, save for the little bit of storytelling he had done. It set Dean's nerves on edge, but there was nothing he could think of to do. Well, besides hope that Mikael would still find a reason to come out this way every now and then, even if it was just for a chat.

"It's about that time," Mikael said finally, his voice soft. He ran his fingers through Dean's hair one last time before standing and making for his truck. Each step the man took brought Dean closer and closer to the reality of the situation. Mikael was leaving, and honestly, Dean didn't know if he was ever coming back. Yet he just sat there, watching the man go.

Mikael stopped as he opened the truck door, turning to stare in Dean's direction, head turned to the side ever so slightly. His face was almost unreadable and what he could read was confusing but intense. Dean had no idea what the other man was thinking.

As he watched Mikael, something brought to mind the strange lupine addition to the farm. Well, the wolf wasn't really an addition, but he did make an appearance now and again. It was enough for him that the beast seemed to have no intent to cause trouble or harm. It would just sit or stand wherever Dean discovered it at night, and watch him. Sometimes it just walked away, back into the woods from where it had come, and other times it waited until Dean walked off of his own accord.

It was absurd, but Dean thought that Mikael's face bore the exact same look as the wolf. It was predatory, sure, but it was also thoughtful, the wondering expression of a primal animal with far more intelligence than most people gave it credit for. Dean couldn't shake the comparison, no matter how utterly ridiculous it seemed. His fingers found the necklace around his neck, twiddling the pendant idly.

He heard a soft snort from Mikael as the man's face shifted to a smile before he waved and hopped into the truck. Dean watched the taillights as they pulled onto the path and headed toward the road. Long after all signs of the truck had faded away, he sat there staring into the night.

Eventually he managed to pick himself up off the step, his chest tight and his heart heavy. It was silly to have gotten so attached to Mikael. The carpenter? Who gets hung up on the strong and sweaty carpenter? The man was just supposed to help him a bit with the repairs he couldn't do by himself. That was it. Their friendship had been a surprise, the sexual attraction a bonus... or a curse. But to let it go further... that was just foolish.

He'd gone to bed pondering that foolishness. He would

bet that Mikael had become aware of his feelings, hence the quiet behavior. It could very well be that he was never coming back, spooked away because Dean had gotten too attached... like a fool. Dean finally went to sleep that night still trying to make peace with the idea that Mikael was never coming back.

The next few days would serve as a test of his resolution on the matter. While he hadn't expected to see Mikael on the road the next day, he found himself hoping he would. As it turned out, the following day was worse for him, and the day after that was more difficult still.

He tried to settle down, even as he threw himself head-long into his work. Chiding himself for even worrying over it was absolutely no help at all, serving only to remind him of his troubles and failings. As stupid as it had been to let himself develop feelings for Mikael, it wouldn't be any less foolish if he gave himself a hard time over it. If anything, it made him melancholy. He missed the other man's ability to make him laugh and brighten his days.

The difficult times stretched beyond those first few days, and he found that it really didn't get much easier. Dean's logical reasons to justify Mikael's failure to return were falling apart. The "busy with another job" rationale failed after the first weekend passed with no visit. Mikael took his weekends off very seriously, and if he'd wanted to come by, he would have. It was a stretch, but Dean even went so far as to say that perhaps he had taken a vacation and would be back before long. That flimsy excuse didn't hold up much longer than midway into the second week.

About the time all the justifications and excuses Dean could come up with had lost their luster, a great depth of sadness hit him. Even if Mikael's feelings didn't mirror his own, he had really believed the other man had cared for him, at least a little. It was hard to believe that he'd misread Mikael so badly and had somehow thought him seriously invested enough to maintain some sort of relationship into the future. Even if it meant no sexual play, and they settled back into just the uncomplicated friendship they'd enjoyed, Dean would have gladly taken it. He was drawn to the man, but it didn't mean that he had to go and slap romance into the mix and expect it to work. Apparently, Mikael had caught wind of it and had decided to get away from the mess while he could.

It took Dean some serious thinking time, and finally, late into the night a few weeks after Mikael left, he reached his conclusion. Mikael wasn't pretending, or rather, hadn't been pretending. If anything, he had been completely genuine, and it wasn't his fault that Dean had gone and added an extra complication to the whole mess. It was more than likely that he knew Dean was feeling this way about him and had decided to keep his distance. Why Mikael thought complete radio silence was the way to go, Dean didn't know or understand.

He would simply have to find a way to get ahold of Mikael and try to explain things to him. There was no reason for their friendship to suffer simply because Dean had feelings for him that went beyond just friends. Dean was a big boy—he could deal with not having what his stupid heart wanted at the moment. Given the chance, he would explain to Mikael how he really felt about the whole situation. Their friendship was far more important than a romantic relationship any day, that was all there was to it.

His thoughts were interrupted by a glint of light in the darkness. Instinct took hold and he froze, realizing how late it was and that he was quite vulnerable, sitting, as he was, on the bottom step of his porch. It wasn't until the light shone again that he recognized the pair of glowing eyes in the dark.

"Hey, haven't seen you in a while, bud," he said as the wolf moved into sight. It stopped to stare at him. "I, uh... thought you had left me, too."

He laughed, almost wishing he could pet the animal. Calm and non-threatening as the animal was, it was still a wolf, and he wasn't stupid. If he wanted to pet something, he'd just cuddle up with Jax. The dog was lying calmly on the other side of the screen door, barely even stirring as the wolf approached. Dean was never quite sure if the dog even knew the wolf was there.

The wolf cocked its head at him, bringing a sad smile to Dean's face. "You look a lot like a friend of mine when you do that, you know?"

A snort was all he received.

"Well, you do. Or at least, I thought he was a friend. Pretty sure I scared him off, though. He hasn't been around for a few weeks, and I'm pretty sure it's my fault."

No response. Not that he had been expecting one.

"I never had many friends, you know? Even growing up I wasn't that good at making them. I wouldn't have minded a few friends now and again, but I guess I just got used to being alone. Then I meet this guy, and we really hit it off. I thought we were going to have a really great friendship. When you come to a quiet place like this, you'll want to have a few people you're close to. Nice as the quiet is, now it seems too quiet without him around."

The wolf didn't sit, instead just shifting slightly, keeping its gaze steady on Dean.

"It's weird to think you have a close friend and then have him just... disappear like that. I think even Jax has looked for him a few times, though it's kinda hard to tell—he's always sniffing around for no reason. So, this guy has a way of taking up a whole space with just his existence, ya know? The whole farm seems too quiet without him out here hammering at something, swearing at the project he's working on, or cracking bad jokes at me across the field."

The animal cocked its head in the other direction but made no further movement.

"Wish I could talk to him. I never was much of a talker, though you probably think I'm lying, since I'm sitting here babbling at you, but it's true. People always seem like they don't care. They're too busy to really listen. They just want something specific from you. They're just passing the time. All sorts of stuff. But he listened, and he talked—like, really talked. It was so easy to open up to him, too, about anything. That's kind of a big thing to find in someone when you've never really been able to talk to people before."

He sighed, feeling spent from the excessive one-sided conversation streak he'd been on. The wolf eyed him with that same curiosity that it always had. Dean would swear it seemed the wolf would have plenty to say if it were given the chance. Either that, or it was really thinking long and hard about something all the time.

"You're a weird animal, I hope you know that," he snorted, waving the animal off. "Go on with you. Go be a normal wolf and go hunt something. Not me, of course, but I guess you would have by now if you were so inclined."

It gave a slight sniff, sounding almost offended. Dean watched it turn and walk off, amused that the animal seemed to listen to him. Hell, for all he knew, the animal could understand him, which probably meant it thought he was a complete idiot by now. Not much could invalidate this either, considering he had just sat here and spilled his guts to an animal. Well, a wild animal—it was totally different when he talked to Jax or Nix, of course.

The whole thing did make him feel a little better, though. Talking out his problems made him feel a little more stable and on an even keel, having gotten it out there into the universe as he had. It made him more resolute in his decision to try and get in touch with Mikael. There was no guarantee that reaching out would make a bit of difference in the long run, but he would kick himself forever if he didn't at least try.

He still had the number for Mikael's boss somewhere in the house. That was as good a place to start as any, and maybe he would get lucky and catch Mikael while he was around. He knew that Mikael didn't have a phone of his own and that there were no phones in The Grove as far as he knew. So, that being the only option available, he had his plan.

First, he would pick himself up from these steps and stop feeling sorry for himself. There would be plenty of time to mope if he didn't succeed in contacting Mikael and get a chance to explain. Come morning, he would make the call. If that didn't work, he would try again, and keep trying... at least until he felt like he was being too annoying or until he managed to succeed.

This was the first sound plan he'd had in a while, and it did wonders for his nerves. It might not work out the way he hoped, but at least it was something to work with. With his nerves settled enough to function, he did in fact pick himself up off the step. He nudged Jax awake and coaxed him upstairs. He glanced toward the half full moon up in the big black sky, and silently prayed that something good would come of this.

9

*I*t would be another week before he had any sort of result from his attempts to contact Mikael. The sound of the familiar truck approaching the house could be heard from his place in the kitchen.

Mikael was jumping down from the cab of the truck just as Dean stepped out onto the porch. For a moment, he could feel his breath catch in his throat as he caught sight of the man. The long, well-muscled body held snugly in his clothes and the flash of those hazel eyes as they looked up at him took his breath away. Even the serious expression on his face was wonderful to see, though his heart was beating a little harder than he wanted it too. Lord, he had to get ahold of himself or he was going to be a mess before he even started. The last thing he needed was to end up a tongue-tied idiot just because his body was betraying him.

"Hey," he said as stepped up onto the porch. For a moment Dean was tempted to sit down on the step as he was used to doing, but he thought better of it. Mikael didn't look exactly at home or like he was going to be staying long.

He hadn't even smiled, not in the slightest. Already, Dean could feel his heart sinking.

"Hey." Mikael's response was quiet, and he shifted a little as he stood in front of the steps.

"How have you been?" Dean asked, feeling his own voice going quiet, and sounding almost meek. He didn't like how unsure he was suddenly feeling. He had felt better this past week, more self-assured, but that confidence was quickly fading with each passing second. Mikael was obviously uncomfortable and clearly didn't want to be there.

"Fine. So, I'm guessing you wanted to talk to me." It wasn't a question.

"Kinda."

"Kinda? You've been blowing up the Old Man's phone every day this week."

Dean winced at the tone of accusation. "Was it that bad?"

Mikael snorted. "Well, now he thinks I screwed up on the job, so he chased me out here to figure out what was going on, since you wouldn't tell him what was wrong."

Dean's gaze fell to his feet, his heart sinking in his chest at the man's words. Mikael hadn't come out to the farm because he'd wanted to—his boss had forced him to. That scored pretty high on the list of things Dean hadn't wanted to hear. Mikael definitely did not want to be here, but Dean had forced his hand. All he could do at this point was to continue with his plan, albeit with considerably less enthusiasm than he had begun with.

"Sorry," Dean sighed. "But ya know, it's been a few weeks. I kinda wanted to explain myself a little."

Mikael eyed him warily. "Explain yourself? About what?"

Dean scoffed. "C'mon, Mikael. If it had been a week or

whatever, I wouldn't even be saying anything. But it's been a bit longer than that. You've been avoiding me completely. That's not so hard to pick up on."

It was Mikael's turn to sigh now, shuffling on the spot. "Look, it's not personal. It's not that I want to avoid you, it's just—"

He was cut off by Dean's raised hand. "Look, I know that you know, okay? I haven't exactly been subtle about it, so... I'm sorry, okay? I know it was just supposed to be some friendship with a little fun sex thrown in. Then I went and started having feelings and getting attached in ways I shouldn't have and all that mess. I know you picked up on it, and I don't blame you for backing away from it once you had the chance, though I wished you would have at least said something first. But that's not really important. What matters is that at the end of the day, I know I can just be friends with you, without all the extra stuff if that's—" Dean faltered at Mikael's utterly stunned expression. "What?"

Mikael's expression shifted to a guarded worry. The fear began to creep up on Dean as he watched the man struggle for a moment with his words. Holy shit, Dean thought. Had Mikael not known at all what he had been feeling? Had he just opened his mouth and made the situation worse than it was to begin with?

"Dean," Mikael began, struggling. "You... Look. It's... It's not that. I... wondered, but that's not why, man. It's really better for you if I don't come around much anymore, okay? I'm not supposed to—"

Now it was Dean's turn to frown. "Your family?"

Mikael glanced up, worry on his face. "Yeah, it's... complicated. I don't wanna drag you into my mess. Bad enough that I was dealing with Town, it's even worse that I made friends with someone for real this time. They don't want me dealing with Town too much, and you're not even Town, you're an outsider. They're just... they're worse than usual, man. I don't want you dragged into this, it can get... bad."

"Because you're friends with me?"

If Mikael hadn't been looking directly at him when he asked the question, Dean probably would have missed the reaction on his face—that anxious pain that Dean knew too well and just how much the man hadn't wanted to be away. Mikael was feeling guilty, but even worse, his face showed a flash of longing. It was gone in the next instant, but Dean had seen it all very clearly.

"You, too?" Dean stepped down before Mikael could question himself. "So, more than just friends, is it?"

Mikael's expression was pained, and it was obvious he was trying to deny the truth. It was equally obvious that he wasn't too pleased that Dean had stepped close. Yet, he seemed even more disturbed at his own failure to step back. Dean wished he could read Mikael's mind at this moment, to know exactly what was going on in there. The only consolation he had was that Mikael hadn't retreated from him, even though he was still eyeing him warily.

"Christ, it's true," Dean breathed.

Dean reached out to take his hand. Mikael tensed and for a moment, Dean thought he might yank his hand back or even bolt. The moment stretched on before Mikael's hand finally relaxed in his own. Mikael made a soft sound that Dean would almost dare call a whimper, as he gave in to the touch and curled his fingers around Dean's hand.

"Fine," Mikael said, pained. "It's true. I wondered if you felt that way, because I was feeling it, too. Being around you has been so... it's... I can't help myself, ya know? I can't help but give in to the feeling when I'm with you, and I don't want... I don't want to be away from you like this, man. It really sucked."

Dean bit his bottom lip. "How did they even find out?"

Mikael shifted uncomfortably, "They have their ways. There's more to The Grove than we let on and my family... well, they're the closest to what you'd call leaders for The Grove. So, knowing stuff about everyone in The Grove is kinda their thing."

"I don't want to get you into worse trouble than you already are..."

That brought a snort from the larger man. "They aren't going to do anything except irritate me. I just don't want you dragged into this mess. I know I keep saying that, but it's true. You don't deserve it."

"But... what if I don't mind?"

"You don't know what you're saying, and that's why you can say that."

Dean paused at that, giving it some actual thought. What he knew about The Grove and its people was rather lacking. He couldn't claim to know what sort of problems would come his way if he were to push for this. Then again, he remembered all too clearly how he felt, and how Mikael apparently felt, and he remembered his grandfather and the man's discussion of paths. Especially those not travelled.

"If... If you weren't worried about that, would you want more?" Dean's heart raced as he asked the question, proud of himself for sounding far calmer than he felt.

There was another pause as Mikael stared at him. "Yes."

Dean smiled, stepping a little closer. "Okay. So, why not?"

Mikael eyed him, still wary. "You say that like it's not a big thing to worry about."

"Maybe it is," Dean admitted, slowly slipping a hand

around Mikael's waist. "I'm not going to stand here and say that I understand exactly what you're worried about. But..."

Mikael gave into the touch, gradually relaxing into the embrace. The worry never left his face, but he relaxed. Dean's heart rate picked up again as he felt Mikael willingly give in to the moment. Mikael was hard against him—in more ways than one. It wasn't difficult to notice the man's cock pressing against him as his fingers found their way under the back of the man's shirt, brushing his warm skin.

"Dean," Mikael said, his pupils dilating, his expression beginning to shift.

"Stay?" Dean whispered, looking up completely to stare at the other man. It was as much a question as it was a statement. They both knew what he wanted from Mikael. Hell, from the way the man didn't fight him, it was obvious that Mikael wanted it just as much. All he needed was for Mikael to stop fighting it and just let them have this. He couldn't figure out what the hell had brought this about for either one of them, but it was here, and it wasn't easily ignored.

Mikael seemed to struggle with his words, unable to form a reply. After a moment, he reached a conclusion in his mind. Strong arms circled around Dean and pulled him in, their bodies flush against one another. Dean only had a moment to stare up into the other man's eyes before Mikael bent his head and gently pressed Dean's mouth with his own.

Heat flashed through Dean at the kiss, his body immediately feeling both electrified and weak. A soft murmur escaped him, and he quickly brought his hand up, entangling his fingers into Mikael's thick, soft hair. Mikael's hand pressed at the small of his back, pulling him in even tighter. The kiss was stronger than the others had been, both men now more honest in their emotion than they had been before. Mikael was as forward and confident as ever but also slow and searching. Dean could feel the man's will against his and he bent to it this time, without a fight.

The air seemed to grow warmer around them as Mikael's hands roamed his body—strong fingers on his back, sliding to his ass, around to his hips. The possessive grip of the man's hands on his hips and ass told him everything he needed to know.

"Upstairs, to my room," he whispered, feeling a little out of breath as he gazed up at the other man.

He wouldn't remember the actual trip up the stairs later, when he tried to recall it all a bit more clearly. Mikael had certainly taken to the suggestion with great vigor. They had somehow managed the path leading into the house and up the stairs. With all their grabbing, fondling, kissing, and gripping, it was a miracle they had made it to the second floor without a single mishap. He did remember quite clearly how the door had flown open before them and how Mikael had made short work of picking him up and chucking him onto the bed with a grunt. Before Dean had recovered from the sudden movement, Mikael was atop him once again.

His fingers fought with the loose button-up shirt that Dean was wearing, but his hurried fingers were unable to undo the small buttons. With a growl that sent a shiver down Dean's spine, Mikael gave up trying. A quick tug and the buttons sprang away from Dean's shirt and clattered onto the floor. Having torn his way to his prize, Mikael latched his warm mouth onto Dean's collarbone, the possessive teeth nipping and drawing a strangled noise from Dean's lips.

As a team, they struggled to remove Mikael's shirt, and for the first time, Dean cursed the tighter shirts that Mikael was so fond of wearing. But soon the man's bare chest was against his, drawing another soft sound of pleasure from Dean as he felt the heat pouring off it. The scent of earth and sawdust—the smell of Mikael—filled his nostrils.

Even as Mikael groped at him, Dean worked just as hard to return the favor. His own hands gripped Mikael's hips, bringing their groins down to grind against each other. Both men groaned at the sudden sensation, thrusting by instinct. Mikael nipped at Dean's bottom lip in response, dragging his teeth along the sensitive skin before claiming his mouth as his own once more. Dean gave in to the dominance, still pulling the man against him.

"Too many clothes," Mikael growled against his mouth.

They began fighting with their jeans. Thankfully, the buttons were far more willing to work with them, and they kicked out of them quickly. The hard length of Mikael's cock hung below him, brushing against the covered length of Dean's own arousal.

"You and your underwear," the man muttered, hooking his fingers into the waistband and jerking them down until Dean's body was free. He didn't have time to respond before Mikael's warm mouth descended, pressing between his groin and inner thigh, teeth scraping against the sensitive flesh. His hips lifted as he gasped, fingers digging into the sheet as Mikael switched sides. The man's tongue ran the length of it, from his balls to the tip of his hard cock.

"God, Mikael. Don't, or I'll—" Dean watched the man's mouth ready to wrap around the head of his cock. He didn't want to cum, not now. He wanted to draw it out and make it last. If the other man went after his cock now, he was sure to lose it.

"Fine," Mikael replied with what Dean could only call a feral grin. "I have another idea, then."

Before he could ask what that was, Mikael's strong hands were on his hips and he was flipped onto his stomach. Work-toughened, warm hands ran down his back, over the curve of his ass, then back up and over his shoulders, fingers strong and searching. Dean could only shiver under the touch.

"Fucking beautiful," Mikael growled. Dean felt his warm breath on his inner thigh. His head bowed forward as Mikael's tongue ran up his leg, across the skin behind his balls, up, and...

"Jesus, Mikael!" he gasped as the man's tongue swept over his sensitive hole. Mikael only hummed in response, his tongue testing and then pressing beyond the ring of muscle. Dean squirmed as the man's tongue pushed into him. He didn't know where the hell Mikael had learned that, but the man's tongue was quickly discovering all the sensitive points inside of him.

He would never own up to the pitiful noises he made as Mikael's tongue swirled inside of him. His hips pressed against the mattress, instinctively seeking the release that he was suddenly craving. It felt like Mikael's tongue was inside him forever, especially after the other man grabbed hold of him and prevented him from grinding against the bed. Pleasure coursed up and down his body as the man's mouth worked.

Mikael's voice came from below as the sensation ceased. "Supplies?"

Dean weakly pointed to the nearby bedside table. "In the drawer."

The other man rolled over and opened it up, pausing. He reached in and pulled out an impressive dildo that he held up for Dean to explain.

Dean chuckled, turning a little pink. "I said I wasn't

getting laid—that doesn't mean I don't like to have a little extra fun when I get off."

Mikael raised a brow, examining the dildo. "Well, at least it means I know you can take me."

"You're a bit bigger than that, but yeah."

He watched the other man pull the condoms and lube out. His breath caught when Mikael hesitated, holding up the condoms with that same cocked brow on his face. Hell, the other man was asking if they really needed them. Dean was fully aware of his own status, of course, even though he had never gone bare with anyone before. He had been too paranoid. Mikael seemed to trust him.

Dean shook his head, "Not if you don't want to."

"Fuck," Mikael grunted, tossing the condoms back into the drawer. "I want to cum inside you, man. Fuck those things."

The man's comment took him from being a little nervous at going bare to full-blown aroused. Now, all he wanted was to feel the other man deep inside him when he came. His comparison of Mikael's cock to the dildo wasn't inaccurate, though. He was going to be feeling it, no matter what.

He had been so lost in his thoughts for a moment, that he hadn't really heard the crack of the bottle opening. It was the cool feeling of lube covered fingers against his hole that brought him back to reality. The sensation of fingers pressing into him drew out a soft gasp as he tried to adjust to the intrusion. The muscles quickly responded, still relaxed from the action of Mikael's tongue just moments ago, Dean let the sensation wash over him.

Mikael took his time, sliding the pair of fingers into Dean, then out again, his other hand resting on the small of Dean's back. His fingers weren't exactly small, and they patiently spread apart inside of him, working against the ring of muscles. Dean knew Mikael was anxious to get moving, and so was he. He pressed back against the man's hand, earning another finger, and felt the sensation of the muscles stretching once more. He groaned into the pillow that he'd buried his face into, still pushing his hips back onto the man's hand. What he really wanted was for Mikael to get it over with and get that cock inside of him.

"You don't quit it, I'm not gonna be patient," Mikael warned with a low gravelly growl.

"Screw patient, just fuck me already," Dean shot back over his shoulder, giving his hips another shove backwards to emphasize his point.

"Your funeral." He pulled his fingers free from Dean's ass. Already missing the feeling of something inside of him —of Mikael inside of him—Dean rocked his ass back in anticipation. The sound of the lube bottle being opened again told him he wouldn't have to wait long. Mikael positioned each of his long legs on either side of Dean before getting himself into position. The blunt tip pressed against his hole, and he felt Mikael brace himself on the bed before pushing forward.

First there was nothing but the pressure against him, then the muscles lost their fight and the head of Mikael's cock slipped in. Dean's gasp drew out into a hiss as the burn hit him. He was thankful the man had gotten as far as three fingers, otherwise that little surprise would have been a lot worse. He felt Mikael pause at his reaction, the man's body tense as he waited to sink into Dean.

Dean wasn't much more patient at this point—what was a little burn? He pushed his hips back onto the man's cock, another few inches slipping into him suddenly, making both men cry out. Dean was determined, pulling his hips forward only to push them back once more. Mikael grabbed his hips, shoving them down into the mattress. He leaned forward now, his breath hot against Dean's neck.

Dean thought Mikael was going to say something but, instead, felt the man push forward. The moan that came from his lips was low and drawn out. Mikael sank into him, rocking back to sink in again, pushing himself into Dean. The press of Mikael's hips against him sent another shiver up his spine. Yeah, he was definitely bigger than the dildo, and Dean couldn't remember ever feeling quite this full.

"Fuck, you're warm," he panted, wriggling under the big man's weight.

Mikael only responded by pulling out about halfway, then shoving back into Dean, wiping out whatever he might have said next. As aggressive and dominant as Mikael had been when they had just been fooling around, it was obvious to a greater degree now. The man had pushed himself back, so that he was once again kneeling behind Dean as he fucked him. The strokes were deep, slower at first but quickly picking up their pace.

Strong hands gripped his waist once more, pulling him back into the thrusts. No one had ever been as deep inside of him as Mikael was at that moment. His ass burned from the sheer strength of the thrusts, pain mingling so wonderfully with pleasure. Mikael filled him again and again, Dean's body jumping under the force of the thrusting.

Dean was beyond words as Mikael fucked him hard, and it seemed the other man was in the same position. Mikael's fingers dug into the skin of his hips, bringing him against his thrusting body with a growl each time. Dean's own cock pressed hard against the mattress, just barely managing to find the friction that he needed. They weren't going to last long like this, but Dean didn't give a shit.

Suddenly, Mikael was pulling out of him, bringing a faint whimper of protest from Dean. The bite of Mikael's nails met his hips, rolling him over again. The man was above him, bringing Dean's legs around his waist. Then the hard cock was inside him once more, the press of the man inside of him, filling him completely.

In this position, Dean could see Mikael's face. It wasn't as deep like this, but it was infinitely better. Mikael's eyes burned into his before the man bent over and claimed his mouth. Every bit of need and hunger poured out of them as their mouths fought. Dean was barely managing to breathe as Mikael's cock and mouth stole his strength from him.

Mikael's position changed again, and Dean cried out, a sudden jolt of pleasure rocking his body. His legs tightened around Mikael's waist, his hands digging into the warm flesh of the man's back. Mikael drove forward again and again, thrusting into the spot that had Dean crying out each time. His cock jumped between them, his body careening toward the inevitable orgasm.

"Cum for me, Dean. Cum with me deep inside of you." Mikael's voice was so unbelievably low. Dean didn't have the strength to wonder at how he had never managed to cum without jerking off first. The man's cock drove into him too damn well for him to muster the strength.

When his orgasm came, it hit him with brutal strength. His body tightened once more around Mikael, the man's name falling from his lips. Warmth pooled onto his upper body as his cock jumped, shooting between their writhing bodies. Mikael's thrusts drove the pleasure through the roof, his body taut as it released.

Above him, Mikael cried out as Dean's body bore down around him, squeezing on the man's cock. All sense of control was stripped from the man, his thrusts now wild and erratic. Through the haze of his orgasm, Dean could swear he felt the man's cock swell even more as he gave a last thrust into him. Mikael's teeth flashed, sinking into the muscles of Dean's shoulder. Both men cried out as Mikael poured into the man beneath him.

When Dean came to his senses, wading through the fog of his orgasm, he realized Mikael had collapsed on top of him. The man's chest rose and fell rapidly, trying to catch his breath. Dean reached up, stroking his fingers through Mikael's damp hair. Low noises came from him, encouraging and soft where his words seemed to fail him. The warmth that filled him completely made his movements languid and gentle.

Mikael roused himself enough to pull free gently from Dean. Dean felt empty as Mikael got up to get them something to clean up with. Dean didn't miss the slight wobble in his steps as he came back. He was a little proud that the man seemed as dazed as he was.

"I can feel it inside me," he finally said, smiling a little.

"It?" Mikael asked as he cleaned Dean's mess from them both.

"Your cum," Dean explained, watching the man's face. "I've never felt that before. It's hot."

Mikael laughed, tossing the used towel to the floor. "Not everyone likes it."

"They're weird." He reached up to pull the man down into a soft kiss. They both made little happy noises that made Dean want to curl his toes almost as much as the other man's cock had. Dean felt... floaty and warm, and the press of the man's body against his was more comforting than arousing at that moment.

"Nap?" Mikael asked as he pulled Dean against him.

Dean nodded, enjoying the feel of Mikael's arms around

him and the breath on his neck. They'd never really been together in a bed, and Dean was pleasantly surprised to find that their bodies curled up perfectly together.

"You going to leave before I wake up?" Dean asked, sleepily.

There was a pause before Mikael answered. "Yes, but I promise you, I'll be back. I'm not going to disappear again."

Dean sighed, but felt a small smile cross his face as he drifted off into the comfort of their shared warmth. Even with that news, he couldn't fight the sheer power of the euphoria flooding his body. Mikael was too warm, too comfortable, and with the rise and fall of his chest, too hypnotizing.

"I believe you."

10

*I*t was the sun that woke him later. His nap had extended into the evening, and the setting sun blazed through his uncovered window. Grumbling, he rolled away from the proximity of the window, flopping to the other side of the bed. It was then that he realized that the other side of the bed was empty. Mikael had left, just as he had said he would.

"Love 'em and leave 'em," Dean grunted, feeling his stomach turn at the thought. He wanted to trust the other man so desperately, and in some strange way, he did. Yet, his mind couldn't quite let go of the idea that perhaps Mikael wasn't being quite as honest as he could be.

It was about that time when he noticed that part of his arm wasn't pressed against the soft sheets of his bed but against something else. A folded piece of paper lay there, now partially crumpled, beneath his outstretched arm. Flipping it around, he saw his own name in handwriting he recognized immediately. As much as it was embarrassing to admit, he had Mikael's handwriting memorized.

"Dean," the note read, "I'm sorry that I left, even though

I told you I'd have to. I *am* coming back, but first I have to deal with my family. I need to know that they won't be a problem for you. I'll be back for you, I promise."

He smiled until his eyes caught the words at the bottom.

"PS: If I'm not back by the weekend, stay in the house at night, just in case." Dean looked up from the paper, perplexed. "Stay inside at night? What the hell is that supposed to mean?"

Jax's head popped up from the side of the bed. Dean held the paper up to the dog. "Any ideas?"

Jax cocked his head, his droopy face sagging to one side, bringing a snort from Dean.

"You know, without all the drooping, that could almost be the same face Mikael makes, sometimes."

The dog barked at the sound of the man's name, hopping excitedly up onto the bed. He began sniffing around, and Dean knew there was no use telling the dog that Mikael wasn't there. The dog would end up combing through one end of the house to the other to find the other man. Only after finally being let out for his last run, would the dog give up the hunt. Dean knew the dog was part boxer, but sometimes he wondered if the dog didn't have some sort of hound in him, too.

Despite his nap, he still felt quite sleepy. This was the first time he had fallen asleep with Mikael in a real bed, and he already felt the loss of his absence. The side of the bed he was pressed against still smelled of earth and sawdust, so he figured he could allow himself the chance to sleep, burrowed in the sheets on that side, and let the alarm wake him in the morning.

It seemed he had barely fallen asleep when the alarm jerked him awake in the morning. After fumbling about with the damn thing and finally turning it off, he glanced about blearily. He hadn't really expected Mikael to be there just yet, especially considering the message. Dreams of running free through woods and meadows had made him think of the man with a faint smile.

It was only after sitting with his morning coffee on the front porch that he had the presence of mind to be concerned. The man had gone out to deal with whatever was going on with his family, in support of the relationship he wanted. Dean still knew very little about Mikael's family, only that there was considerable tension there. He was getting the feeling that Mikael's family was going to be furious that Mikael was dating a guy let alone dating anyone from Town. He could easily picture a small community having an issue with one of their own sons dating another man.

"Wait," Dean suddenly said aloud in the morning air. "If they only like people in their little circle to be together then..." The thought made him crinkle his nose. Obviously, they had to marry outside of the community, otherwise it would get... weird.

Realizing that his thoughts were taking him places he had no business going, he picked himself up from the porch and set himself to work. Industry made the time pass by more quickly, he had long since discovered. Between checking the crops, minding the cows and milking them, chasing chickens back to their rightful place, and all other manner of maintenance, he was kept fairly busy each day.

The first days weren't too bad. After the past few weeks of not even seeing the man, or hearing a word from him, this was an improvement. Mikael had gone out of his way to reassure Dean that he was coming back, so Dean was doing his best to hold it together and not assume the worst. The dull ache in his ass was a pleasant reminder of the man, and the scent left behind in the sheets might last him another night, if he was lucky.

As the week began to pass by, he thought everything over as carefully as he could. One time of having slept with the man had been enough to seal the deal for Dean. After a couple of nights, the faint traces of Mikael had disappeared from his home. Even the faint ache in his body had faded away, leaving him alone with his thoughts. He supposed he should have been frustrated with himself, feeling halfway down the road to being some lovestruck idiot. Yet he couldn't help the smile that came to his lips when he thought about Mikael's eventual return.

Sure, he had his doubts about the other man returning, but he couldn't really blame himself for those concerns either. This time, he felt that the other man was going to stick to his promise. Just as he had somehow known that something was wrong and that Mikael wasn't coming back before, this time he knew he would be coming back.

The only break in the time alone on his farm had been another visit from Mrs. Williams. She was armed with a chocolate pie and apologies for having taken so long in bringing it to him. They chatted a bit while he ate. He beamed when she said that he seemed to be looking better than he had before. He wasn't about to tell her the reason, not only because that would mean explaining a few things about his personal life but also because it would involve bringing up Mikael. He wasn't about to give the woman another chance to have a fit over the matter. So he kept his mouth shut and played the mystery man until she left with a smile and wave.

The pie hadn't even lasted till the weekend. Dean had consumed the whole thing a little more quickly than he would have liked. It had made things a little more enjoyable as the week wore on. There was no such thing as having a total day off when you worked on a farm, but he allowed himself a more relaxed schedule on the weekends. All he really had to deal with were the animals, and even they seemed generally lazy when the weekends came around. Somehow, he had managed to teach the animals that the weekends were for loafing.

He had hoped Mikael would show up by Saturday, but there was no sign of the man, not even a word from him. Instead, he spent his evening alone with Jax curled up in his lap as he sat on the front porch, slowly drinking a beer. The house was dark, and the night sky was lit by the full moon overhead and the twinkling stars around it. It was only then that he wished he had found some reliable way of keeping in contact with Mikael. The anticipation of returning to the bright warmth from everything that had happened the weekend before still sustained him. It wasn't hard to miss Mikael's ready smile or the adorable way he would cock his head when he found something interesting. There was plenty to miss, even if it was only the feel of the man behind him as they lay together.

Jax jerked in his lap, pulling him from his depressing thoughts with a start. He frowned at the animal, wondering what had him staring so intently. Following the dog's gaze into the dark brush beyond the yard, there was nothing that he could see, but then again, he didn't have the same acute sense of smell or hearing that the canine did.

Before he could think to grab the dog, Jax jumped off his lap with a snarl that Dean had never heard before, and he'd had Jax since the dog was eight weeks old. Jax quickly sped out of sight into the dark brush, barking more fiercely. For a brief moment, Dean thought that perhaps his little wolf friend had returned. But then again, Jax had never reacted like this when the wolf had been there before. Hell, Jax had only reacted to any animal's presence with curiosity and interest, never with any degree of ferocity and anger.

The sounds of another snarl had him flying off the porch toward the darkness. His heart pounded in his chest as he pushed through the branches in his path, desperate to find Jax. Tearing through the underbrush and tree limbs, he emerged into a small break in the trees. Every hair on Jax's body stood on end as he bared his fangs at a wolf.

It wasn't the same wolf as before, Dean could see that right away. The wolf was about the same size, which was huge, but its pure black coat identified him as a different animal. The fact that it was snarling furiously at Jax was another sign.

Before he could do much more than feel a tremor of fear run through him, for both himself and his pet, the animals moved. Jax sprawled as the larger beast sent him tumbling into the dirt with another deep, throaty snarl. The dog was up quickly and narrowly missed being caught in the strong jaws as they flashed toward him. Jax, a domesticated animal, stood no chance against a wild wolf. He faintly recalled hearing that the jaws of a wolf could snap a human femur.

A sharp yelp pierced through his panicky haze. The wolf had managed to get his teeth into the dog, and blood now shone on the dog's leg as it limped back with another whimper. All it took was a glance at the wound and the look in Jax's eyes to get Dean moving. Without a thought, he grabbed a hefty fallen branch from the ground, advancing as the wolf moved in for the kill. The wolf darted forward, deadly teeth exposed, and he swung the branch with all the force he could muster. Catching the wolf under the chin, he sent the animal sprawling away from Jax.

"Stay the fuck away from my dog!" Dean shouted,

raising the branch again and hoping he looked braver than he felt at the moment.

The wolf recovered quickly, shaking its head as it stood to face Dean. Now, its fangs were bared, and Dean realized the full danger of the situation. He had definitely pissed it off, and from the looks of the gash on its jaw, he had caused some damage.

It leapt before Dean could formulate a plan. He barely managed to evade. The wolf soared past him, landing in the dirt and turning for the next attack. Dean managed to swing once more, backing the animal off from its next charge. But the next second it charged again, only to duck back from the next swing. This was repeated, frustrating Dean even as it terrified him. It was only after a few more attempts that he realized what the wolf was doing. He couldn't keep swinging this heavy branch forever, but the wolf could keep goading him into swinging it. Hell, it was wearing him down quickly. Were wolves really that smart?

Another feint, and then another, and Dean realized he was right. The wolf wasn't even really trying to get at him, but Dean had no choice but to swing every time it advanced. He tried to back away, to loop around the trees and use them as a shield. The problem was that if he went any further, he would expose Jax, who was in no shape to fight. Dean couldn't carry the dog, either. He would be vulnerable if he tried to pick up Jax, and carrying him would slow him down too much to even attempt an escape.

The simple tactic employed by the wolf was working, and the branch was quickly beginning to feel like a log. He stumbled on one swing, almost tripping over Jax, who was on the ground behind him, still attempting to growl when he could, whimpering when he could not. The wolf finally took the chance, darting beneath the branch, slamming into Dean and knocking him to the ground.

Before he could scramble out of the way to catch his breath, the weight of the animal was on him. Shoving his arms forward, he managed to catch the jaws of the wolf with the branch he somehow still held. His face and throat were spared the grip of the teeth as they sank into the branch instead. The wolf tried to pull back, only for Dean to shove the branch forward, following the animal's movements. Dean knew that so long as the wolf was unable to get its mouth free from the branch, he would be safe. The moment his mouth was free was the moment Dean would find out just how strong those jaws really were. A detached part of his brain noticed that the tear on the wolves' jaw was no longer there, though fresh blood matted the fur all the same.

The wolf now gripped the branch in its teeth. Jerking its head sideways, it tore the wood from Dean's hand. Flailing his arms in the close quarters under the wolf, he tried to kick backwards, but one hand caught in his necklace, snapping the chain and tangling around his fingers. Both hands now free, he scrambled to get away, but the wolf advanced, fangs bared and growling low. Dean braced for the lunge, shoving his hands forward as the animal moved, in a desperate attempt to hold the wolf off. One hand slammed into its forehead, the other against its muscular throat. His arms threatened to buckle under the weight and force of the wolf's power.

A shriek from the wolf caught him off guard. A sizzling patch of burning fur lit up on the wolf's forehead. Bewildered, Dean stared at the patch of blackened fur, almost a perfect circle in shape. His eyes fell to his hand, the one that had hit the wolf's forehead, and he saw it—the glint of the pendant, the same mark on the beast.

Before he could even wonder about the bizarre turn of events, the wolf was quickly recovering. The snarling told him he was in for it now. Frantically, he held up the necklace, some part of him instinctively knowing it was vital to his survival. The wolf eyed the necklace, and the horrible noise that came from its throat was even worse than before.

"Screw you," Dean heard himself say, feeling more angry than afraid, now. He didn't know what the hell was going on, why this animal was even attacking them, or why the freaking necklace had somehow burned the hell out of it. What he did know was that his dog was badly hurt, and his own body was bruised and marked from the fight. This asshole of an animal was trying to kill them, and that just pissed him off.

The wolf bent slightly, leaping toward him. Dean's muscles tensed for another blow just as a blur of brown barreled into the leaping animal. Once again, the black wolf lay sprawled on the ground, this time having suffered a more significant strike than any Dean had managed to inflict. Now fully aware of the second wolf, Dean braced himself for another attack. Suddenly, the familiar light coloring caught his eye.

"Holy shit, seriously?" he cried.

That same patient gaze turned to him, the entire face revealed in the cascading light of the moon. Its head cocked at him, tipping slightly as it took in Dean's haggard state. Dean could clearly see the intelligence in the wolf's face, and he would swear there was concern in those... beauti-ful... hazel... eyes. For a moment, they stared at one another, Dean's eyes widening slowly. His hand rose up before him, the twinkling of the necklace in the moonlight making his eyes even wider.

"Silver," he muttered, his voice filled with wonder as the thoughts bubbled up in his mind, against his will and against all logic. The old stories echoed in his mind, stories he had scoffed at, and still desperately wanted to deny. A full moon, wolves that were larger than they ought to be, and more intelligent than he thought possible. The burning mark from a simple silver pendant. But most of all, he knew those eyes—he knew those eyes so well. How could they be the same? He had stared thoughtfully into those eyes way too many times, too many times to ever mistake them for anything but what they were... who they were. "Mikael?"

The wolf's tail flipped a few times in an unmistakable wag. Dean's jaw dropped, the full realization of what was happening slamming into him. Reality flooded over him, surreal in the revelations it brought home. Numbly, he watched the black wolf pull itself up and lunge at Mikael.

There was none of the subtlety or guile that the black wolf had shown when trying to take Dean down. This was pure animal savagery, mixed with enough human understanding to make the fight quick and bloody. They were evenly matched—both were scoring hits.

Dumbly, Dean sat there watching the fight, arms limp at his sides. The wolves tumbled, rolling around the small clearing, trying to go for the softer, more vulnerable points on the other. Dean couldn't make out who was winning. They were so entwined, he could barely tell one from the other.

"Holy shit," he repeated aloud, still in shock. All those old stories—hell, even the urban legends people had been telling the world over—they were all true? Had this been what Mrs. Williams was talking about? Had this been why

Mikael was so worried all this time? Worried enough to give up on their relationship to protect him? Was the moon really a big deal in the middle of it all, or was it just a coincidence? Some part of Mikael was still awake inside that wolf body, but how much? Did it matter? What could he do? Had the silver really burned that other wolf?

The silver!

He was on his feet and holding the silver chain between his hands before he fully realized what he was doing. The black wolf had managed to get the upper hand, pinning Mikael beneath him. Mikael wasn't giving up that easily, snapping at the other wolf every time it made a move. It was only a matter of time before the black wolf managed to score a blow that would end the fight.

The anger from before boiled up again, this time surging into full-blown rage. Now this asshole, who was also probably just a person under that fur, was trying to kill Mikael. With all of that burning like a brand in his mind, he rushed forward without a thought for his own safety.

How he managed it, he would never be able to describe afterwards. His body landed on the back of the large animal, and the chain slipped over the animal's muzzle and around its neck. This close, Dean could hear the sizzle as he pulled it tight. The wolf gave shocked yelps of pain, jerking backward to shake Dean off. Somehow, he managed to stay on, holding tight as the chain dug into the neck of the giant beast.

The wolf bucked and thrashed, backing up as it tried to throw the crazed human off its back. Dean wasn't letting go until he was thrown off or somehow unable to hold on. The smell of burning hair and skin filled the air, choking him, but he held on. This beast had made his night a living hell, and he wasn't quitting until it did, too.

It flopped, taking Dean with him as it writhed on the ground. Dean was forced to roll away. Only now could he see the smoke rising up off the black wolf, the thick fur around its neck charred and ruined. Mikael, fur dirty and covered in blood, stepped forward as the other wolf managed to dislodge the chain from its neck.

Mikael bent his head near the other animal's stomach, his razor sharp teeth bared near the soft flesh of the belly. The black wolf froze, not daring to move, it seemed. A low rumble came from Mikael's throat, an obvious threat. Slowly, the black wolf, as if not completely ready to commit to the act, rolled onto its back. Dean knew enough about wolf body language to know what that meant. Apparently, it sufficed, and the black wolf was able to stand up, though it did so slowly.

It backed up, eyes locked on Mikael. When its gaze flipped over to Dean, the lip curled up to expose a long sharp fang. Mikael snarled and the wolf darted off into the woods and quickly out of sight.

Dean lay there for what felt like the longest time, reaching forward to pick up the broken chain. The pendant had remained on the chain, somehow. He had been expecting burned skin and fur, but the chain was free of both. Nothing but dirt and a little blood. He slid it into his pocket, sending silent thanks up to wherever his grandfather was, for making sure that thing had somehow found its way to him. Nearby, he saw the wolf containing the man he knew so well.

"It's really you, isn't it?" Dean asked.

There was only a jerk of the head as a response, and Dean sighed.

"I... uh—" He couldn't think of what to say next and

didn't get the time to really figure it out. The faint noise of another pitiful whine alerted him. "Shit!"

Jax whined again, picking his head up to lick his master's hand, as Dean approached. Dean winced as he eyed the ugly wounds, the blood still oozing around them. It looked awful and his throat tightened at the sight.

"I have to get the vet out here," he said, realizing he had no idea where to even find one. Carefully, he picked up Jax, murmuring softly to him as he cradled the dog in his arms. "I got you, buddy. Daddy's got you. We're gonna get you all better, okay? Okay?"

Barely noticing that Mikael was already gone, he stumbled back in the direction of the house, hoping that he wasn't too late to save his best friend.

11

The sun broke over the horizon before Dean's thoughts calmed down enough that he wasn't quite as unsettled. Despite feeling like his nerves were about to leap out of his body at any moment, he had still brewed himself a huge pot of strong coffee. There was no way that he was going to be getting any sleep anyway. Hell, it was probably going to be a coffee-powered day, so he might as well be honest with himself and start it off right.

He felt, more than heard, Mikael come up behind him as he stood at the counter, staring out of the window. For a moment, he expected the man's hands on him, but there was nothing. Dean couldn't really blame him. There was a lot between them that needed to be addressed. Still, he wouldn't have minded Mikael's touch.

"Jax?" Mikael's soft voice was a few feet behind him.

Dean turned around to face him. Wherever Mikael had gone, it had involved getting clothes but, apparently, not shoes. Jeans and a t-shirt, that was all, and Dean could see that the t-shirt didn't fit quite like his others did. For a moment, he wanted to ask where Mikael had stolen them from, but he paused. The man's face was tight, and dark circles hung under his eyes. Mikael seemed as stressed and upset as he felt.

"He's okay now," Dean breathed, feeling the tension easing a bit at the words. "The vet got him patched up and a little drugged. He's got a lot of stitches, and he'll be really sore, but he's gonna be okay. The fun part will be that cone he's got on his head now. He was a terror after I had him fixed—he's not gonna be happy when he wakes up enough to realize he's wearing that stupid thing again."

Mikael cracked a smile at that. "Guess you'll need to hide the breakables."

"Not much left for him to break," Dean sighed. "He's dangerous where fragile stuff is concerned, even when he's not wearing a cone."

Mikael chuckled, the noise trailing off after a moment and ending abruptly. The tension hung between them again, each of them waiting for the other to break the silence. Dean watched Mikael, trying to make up his mind about whatever was going on in his head. His eyes fell on the man's left shoulder and forearm where they were wrapped in bandages.

"The other... uh, wolf... it seemed like he healed really fast after I smacked him with that branch," Dean finally said, unable to contain himself.

Mikael nodded. "Yeah, we, uh... We heal pretty fast."

"Then why—?"

"Some things don't heal that well," Mikael said, glancing down with a shrug. "Like the teeth of our own kind."

"Or silver?" Dean asked.

"Yeah, or silver. Other stuff does it, too, but those are the two biggest things."

Dean sighed, looking up at the ceiling. "Full moon?"

Mikael laughed at that. "We can turn any time, actually. The full moon just... I don't know how to explain it. You want to turn when the moon is full and up high, it's like... Kinda like how, deep down, I wanna touch you. Or when I do touch you, I want more, I want to feel you... more of you. It's a..."

"A primal thing?"

"Yeah, that's exactly it. That's the best way to put it."

Dean wanted to smirk but could only sigh, taking in the information. He had spent a great deal of the past few hours thinking over everything that had happened. It was difficult to say exactly how he felt about the whole thing, though the shock had worn off. Now, he was full of questions for the other man.

"So, that was really you as a wolf this whole time, coming over here onto my property?" he asked, despite knowing the answer already.

"I wanted to keep an eye on you. I couldn't help it."

Dean could smile at that. In truth, the idea that the other man had gone out of his way to be there, around him, warmed him a little. He supposed he should have been a little creeped out, or at least annoyed, for a while. Mikael had led him to believe he was gone for good. Maybe he was just too tired to be really annoyed over it, or maybe he was just weird. "So, you decided to just... freak me out a few times instead? I mean really, you just pop up outta nowhere, full blown wolf? Were you trying to freak me out?"

Mikael flushed. "No, that wasn't it at all. Just like I said before, the whole full moon thing makes the desire to change hard to resist. But when you're a wolf... well..."

"Well, what?"

Mikael took a deep breath, steadying himself, "When you're a wolf, you're different. The human is still there, but so is the wolf. It's always there really, even now, but it's a lot stronger when you're in that form. Wolf instincts are strongest when the moon is full. My wolf half wanted to see you for itself, when it was free, and so—"

"Wait, so it's always there, always-always?"

"Yeah. It's a part of me. And always has been."

"Two spirits," Dean muttered, thinking back to the story he had told Mikael. How bizarre to think that he had thought he'd been telling Mikael a fascinating tale, a mythology of sorts, when the man probably knew it already, as fact. Life really was strange. "Wait, does that mean your whole family is…?"

Mikael winced at that. "It's not… all of us. It's a genetic thing. If two… uh—"

Dean raised a brow. "Might as well say 'werewolves' and get it over with. The cat—or wolf, to be accurate—is out of the bag now."

Mikael continued with a faint smile. "Right. If two werewolves have kids, the chance of the kids being one, too, is high but not guaranteed. Hell, two humans can make one and not even know it. We don't show the full signs of it until we're close to our first change. It's good if it's in a werewolf family, or community, but sometimes it happens in human families where the parents don't know they even carry the genes, much less that they passed them on. That can be… really messy."

Dean didn't have to wonder, but he asked anyway. "Messy?"

"Changing for the first time is a terrifying experience, even if you know what's happening. All of a sudden, your body is changing, totally. You're becoming an animal and that animal is right there in your head. People tend to lose it the first time they change, even when they've been warned.

Others? They can go feral sometimes, but they usually leave a mess behind them first."

"So, it's just genetic then? Not the whole 'two spirits' thing that I brought up?"

"Sorta? I don't really know too much about it, but there are people in The Grove who know the stories better. They know what we are a lot better than I do. I never did care much about all that. I just wanted to live my life. But I'd say it's both, spirit affecting flesh and the other way around."

Again, all Dean could do was nod, mulling the new details over in his head. He'd never been much for pondering spiritual matters. What interest he'd ever had in the past died with his family years ago. He could certainly understand wanting to go your own way, but hadn't Dean wanted the same thing for himself? The difference was that Dean had held himself back all those years. Mikael apparently had a whole slew of people, especially his family, standing in the way of him living life as he pleased.

Family. Another thought came to Dean. "And that other one? The black wolf?"

Mikael frowned. "My cousin."

Dean stared. "Your cousin? He attacked me!"

Mikael looked troubled. "I know. I don't know if that was what he meant to do or if he just wanted to scare you and it got out of hand. But it was definitely what he was trying to do when he got pushed, so yeah, I guess."

Dean gave a low whistle at that. "You weren't kidding about your family stuff being complicated, were you?"

"No, I wasn't. I'll have to face them all again at some point but..."

Dean turned, pouring another cup of coffee and wishing it was beer instead. After a pause, he pulled another cup from the cupboard and poured one for Mikael. The man clearly hadn't slept, either, what with being up all night saving Dean's ass. Mikael seemed grateful for the coffee, sipping it with a slight grimace, which made Dean laugh. He really had brewed it strong.

The laugh seemed to lighten the tension slightly. He looked at Mikael. "What else is different?"

Mikael looked up from his coffee. "Different?"

"Yeah, me being human, you being... a werewolf." He paused for a deep breath and then continued, "What else makes you different from me? I mean, you can turn into a wolf, which is pretty handy. Silver sucks for you. I'm guessing you can probably sense stuff better than me, if I think back a bit. And does being one... alter you... ya know, *physically*, too?"

Mikael looked at Dean, eyeing him with a deadpan expression of his own. "Are you asking me if being a were-wolf makes me have a big dick?"

A sharp bubble of laughter escaped from Dean's throat. "Maybe?"

"Trust me, that has nothing to do with it. Rest assured, there are plenty of little dicks out there."

That comment only caused Dean to laugh even harder, forcing him to set his coffee down before he spilled it. The laughter seemed to force its way out of him as he doubled over, unable to contain it. The tension and fear of the past several hours came out as overblown, ridiculous laughter. It wasn't long until Mikael was behind him, laughing as well, though not as hard. He was laughing at Dean rather than the crazy situation, but both men couldn't help but be swept up in the moment of sheer lunacy.

Eventually, Dean was able to stand, wiping the tears of laughter from his face. His life had been a wild ride for years now, even if there were periods of peace. Now, he was standing in the kitchen with a bona fide werewolf, a werewolf he happened to find breathtaking. Even with the bags under his eyes, the bandages, and the stiffness in his shoulders, the man was one of the most beautiful things Dean had ever seen.

He reached forward, cupping Mikael's face and smiling. "Did you really mean it? Wanting to be with me, I mean?"

Mikael's face went serious, his free hand coming up to cover Dean's. He searched Dean's face, his fingertips warm against Dean's hand. This simple act of touching brought a sense of calm to Dean's mind. There was still a world of things to address, but for now, he had Mikael with him, and that was all that mattered.

"I meant it, and I still mean it," Mikael said. "If you still want me, anyway."

Both Mikael's tone and his face showed the bald fear that he had been feeling. Dean could see the worry etched on every part of him. Poor Mikael had been keeping this secret from the world for his whole life, and had even been keeping it from Dean the entire time they'd been friends. It was one hell of a secret, Dean couldn't deny that, but...

There was still plenty to work through, and Dean still felt like his head might spin right off of his shoulders at any point. But could he really turn Mikael away now? He wasn't even bothered by the secret-keeping—it was one hell of a fact to lay at someone's feet. If Dean hadn't seen it for himself, he would have thought that Mikael was lying to save face, or to spare Dean's feelings. It would have been the strangest lie he'd ever heard, but he would have believed it to be a lie, nevertheless. Turns out seeing really was believing.

There was quite a gulf of information that he had yet to be told, and even more he had to understand completely. It wasn't often that someone found out that everything they'd believed about the world wasn't completely true. It left a lot of questions about other myths and legends, including the ones his grandfather used to tell.

He knew Mikael was worried. It was quite a bombshell that had blown up in Dean's face, and he knew the other man was beyond freaked at the possible consequences. Dean would be drawn into his world, no matter how much they tried to avoid it.

Yet, Mikael had stuck by him, even if it had been in a way that Dean hadn't known about at the time. Mikael had followed through on his word and even saved his life, exposing everything about himself and widening the rift between himself and his family. He had already risked so much and was risking more by telling Dean all of this. Mikael had sacrificed, yet was still standing here, looking vulnerable and afraid.

"You're a pretty wolf," Dean said. Mikael blinked in surprise, then turned a dusty shade of pink.

It was the flush that did it for Dean. The rush of color to the other man's face, coupled with the undiluted embarrassment he obviously felt, was too sweet and endearing. Dean leaned forward, cupping his hand behind Mikael's head to pull him down into a kiss. It was all just as before, the tightening of his stomach muscles, the rush of heat that threatened to melt him, and the smell of the man filling his nose, soothing him into a peaceful bliss.

"Yeah," Dean whispered against the man's lips.

"Yeah? You'll...?" Mikael asked breathlessly.

Dean's eyes lit up, his thumb tracing Mikael's jaw. "Yeah."

EPILOGUE

*H*ad it really only been a week since so much of what he'd always believed about the world had been turned on its head?

He didn't know just how much of his grandfather's stories were actually true. But there was enough truth there to make him wonder about the rest of it, for sure. To see for himself the tales of beasts in human form coming to life had boggled his mind. He was still trying to process the whole thing, and at times was more than a little taken aback by one thing or another that he learned. Yet, the fact that he was head over heels crazy over one of them was even more preposterous.

Maybe it was just the fact that he was crazy over a guy in general that was strange to him. Who knew?

Mikael hadn't left the property since the morning after the fight and subsequent revelations. Dean felt as though the other man might have been waiting for the other shoe to drop, perhaps for Dean to realize what he was really getting into and boot him out without a second thought. That, or maybe the man was just feeling terribly guilty. He certainly seemed to dote over Jax while the dog was recovering, as if the injuries were somehow his fault. Dean watched the two of them, feeling his chest squeeze. It was sweet to see this big, scary man with the kindest eyes coo and whisper to the slow and pitiful dog as it tried to wiggle against him. Mikael even insisted on applying the medicine to the dog's wounds, being gentler than Dean ever thought possible.

Maybe Dean would hit a wall and decide he couldn't take what happened, that he couldn't believe this was happening, and wanted nothing to do with it. But he didn't think so. There was too much goodness here for him to turn his back on it.

Moments like watching Mikael with Jax. Like watching the man's silhouette moving against the backdrop of the setting sun. Hearing him hum to himself as he cooked them dinner. Seeing him smile whenever Dean entered the room. Feeling the warmth of his body pressed against him when they slept, eager to feel Dean against him, no matter what.

The fact that the sex was continuing to blow his mind certainly didn't hurt matters, either.

Nothing could have prepared him for where his life had already taken him over the past handful of months. Finding the legacy his grandfather had left to him. Taking the chance to step out of his dismal existence and throw himself, and everything he had, into this place. Meeting Mikael and making a real friend for the first time in so long. Then working through the complications, the feelings, the sexual aspects, and everything else that served to muddy the waters.

How funny it was to him to think that those were his concerns only a week ago. Now, he realized they were nothing in comparison to now.

Everything either of them had dealt with before had

been done separately. Neither of them had gone through this life untouched or scar-free. Yet, now they each had the other by their side to work through whatever came their way. He didn't really know what those situations could be, but he knew that Mikael was willing to brave with him.

Dean knew it wasn't going to be as easy as all that. He still had plenty to learn, plenty to digest. He was a human being, Mikael was a werewolf. A fact he found out the hard way, if there was such a thing. Was there an easy way to discover something like this? A whole new reality had opened up before him in such a short amount of time. Who knew what else was coming his way?

Mikael would eventually have to face his family. Everything that had happened meant that he was going back to one hell of a storm. Dean hadn't yet got into what the werewolf family was like, or what their politics were, but he was betting it would get messy. Mikael seemed in no rush to face whatever the consequences would be from his family, so Dean was just happy to have him around.

This was what he found himself thinking as he watched Mikael walk across the yard toward the porch. The man's eyes found him, and he waved. Dean sighed happily as he watched his approach. The sight of the man never ceased to both stimulate and relax him. Watching his muscles move beneath his clothes, the way his eyes fell so confidently on Dean as he grew nearer. It was a strange mix of arousal, and a surge of emotions that always seemed to rattle him inside. It was terrifying and exhilarating.

"I'm going to have to see my family soon. You know that, right?" Mikael asked, stopping before Dean and staring down at him.

Dean returned the stare. "You mean 'we,' right? *We* have to go see your family soon."

"Not letting that go, are you?"

"Nope." Dean took the other man's hand. "We're going together. It's only right. You're not facing this alone, not when I'm the reason for it."

"That isn't fair, and you know it's dangerous."

"Maybe. Probably."

"Probably?" Mikael asked in disbelief. "They're gonna be pissed when I show up and doubly will be pissed if I bring you along. I'm afraid they'll take all their frustrations out on you, Dean. I don't want you getting hurt over this. Jax already got hurt because one member of my family came out here over this. I don't want to drag you over there and deal with them all directly."

"Hey, Mikael?"

Mikael hesitated, before finally sighing. "Yes?"

"Ignore all that. Pay attention to *that*, instead."

Dean motioned to the setting sun. Mikael glanced at the sunset, then down at the other man before finally laughing.

"Touché."

Dean could only smile as the man settled in next to him on the swing. The press of his body against him made the colors of the sunset even more beautiful. Sure, it was sappy, but it was the kind of sappy he could learn to live with. He was allowed to be sentimental, in his opinion. With so much going on, all he could do was soak up the sweet moments like this. Somehow, he felt like they would come in handy a little later when it all hit the fan, as it most surely would.

So yeah, the future was right around the corner. It was filled with a bunch of pissed off werewolves that were probably going to want a piece of one, or both, of them. The events that would follow all of this were bound to be interesting, like the old Chinese curse falling onto their lives. For all the downs that were most likely coming their way, he wanted to cherish the ups. On the farm, they were cut off from the outside world, at least temporarily. As soon as they stepped back into reality, he was pretty sure reality would come crashing down with a vengeance.

"Totally worth it," he murmured to the air, taking Mikael's hand in his own, content to just enjoy the sunset before them.

Made in the USA
Lexington, KY
13 April 2018